the further adventures of

SHERLOCK HOLMES

THE INSTRUMENT OF DEATH

T0371885

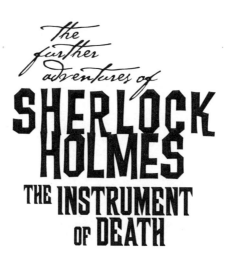

the further adventures of SHERLOCK HOLMES
THE INSTRUMENT OF DEATH

DAVID STUART DAVIES

TITAN BOOKS

THE FURTHER ADVENTURES OF SHERLOCK HOLMES:
THE INSTRUMENT OF DEATH
Print edition ISBN: 9781785658488
E-book edition ISBN: 9781785658495

Published by Titan Books
A division of Titan Publishing Group Ltd
144 Southwark Street, London SE1 0UP

First Titan edition: February 2019
10 9 8 7 6 5 4 3 2 1

What did you think of this book? We love to hear from our readers. Please email us at: readerfeedback@titanemail.com, or write to Reader Feedback at the above address.

To receive advance information, news, competitions, and exclusive offers online, please sign up for the Titan newsletter on our website: **www.titanbooks.com**

To Michael Daviot and Mark Kydd.
The new brilliant portrayers of Holmes and Watson.

Prologue

He looked up at the night sky, a smile forming on his lips as he observed the full moon emerging in all its radiant glory from behind a bank of grey clouds, glowing brightly in the indigo heavens. He was mesmerised by it. Unfettered by the ragged clouds, the moon was there now to observe him, to support him, to bear witness, to shed its creamy light on his dark deed. It was as though it were his luminous confederate. He raised his hand to his forehead in gentle salute. The moon had given him its blessing and now he could be about it. Now he could proceed with the murder. Now he could kill.

Chapter One

Even as a child, Gustav Caligari had been an odd individual. A large baby, he had developed into a sturdy toddler, much bigger than his confederates at kindergarten. At this early age he was already an intimidating presence, which made it easier for him to bully and manipulate his peers. He was alone with his father in the city of Prague, his mother having succumbed to typhoid shortly after the child's birth. The boy's father, Emeric Caligari, taught surgical technique at the Charles-Ferdinand University in the city and his demanding duties left him little time for his son. In truth, he had no real interest in the child following the death of his wife. The boy was a constant, painful reminder of his loss and so he left the domestic parenting duties to the hired nanny, Rosa Placzek, sending the boy from home during the day as soon as feasible.

Despite his size, Gustav Caligari was a quiet creature, but he harboured a dark, sadistic nature. Even before the age of five he had developed a fascination with the torture of small animals and insects. He would trap a group of spiders in a jar, drop a lighted taper into their midst and chuckle with glee as the tiny limbs writhed and shrivelled in the flames. His favourite trick was to catch a small bird, a sparrow or a wren, and slowly twist its head round until he heard the tiny bones snap, finally tearing it off, delighting in the furious flapping of the wings and the twitching of the bird's body until life in the mutilated creature ebbed away.

On one occasion Rosa Placzek caught him trying to strangle a kitten. He seemed surprised and annoyed when she shouted at him, snatching the terrified animal from his grasp. He failed to understand why she was so angry, why she remonstrated with him at length and called him "a devil child". To his mind, he had merely been exercising his curiosity. He was experimenting, he explained simply and unemotionally. He only wanted to see how long the kitten would struggle before it surrendered itself to death. His mother had abandoned him and he wondered how hard she had fought to stay.

When Gustav began formal schooling at the age of five, he turned his attention to his fellow pupils. Larger and stronger than his contemporaries, he always targeted the weaker, less intelligent children, carefully finding a time when he could lure them away to some isolated spot. Then he would subject them to bouts of bullying: biting their arms, poking them in the eye and on one occasion bringing a large stone down on another boy's foot, breaking many of the delicate bones.

This incident resulted in Gustav's removal from the school.

"I am sorry to inform you that your son has serious problems," the headmaster informed Gustav's father, who had been summoned to his office. "He has an inability to integrate peacefully with the other children and he seems consumed with a desire to hurt them. What is so chilling is that he carries out these terrible acts in what appears to be a calm and matter-of-fact manner. He never seems angry or loses his temper. It is almost as though he causes pain purely in a spirit of enquiry. To him they are experiments in torture. This is a most disturbing trait and I suggest that you seek medical advice and treatment. This dark tendency should be nipped in the bud. If not..." The headmaster shook his head.

Emeric had no doubts. Quite clearly, his son was a monster in embryo.

After Gustav's removal from public education, a series of private tutors came to the house, the majority of whom lasted only a few months. These frustrated pedagogues found the boy a conundrum. On the surface he was polite and docile with rare flashes of charm, but he was also monosyllabic and rarely responded to any of the stimuli they provided.

That was until Hans Bruner appeared on the scene.

In many ways, he was a last resort. Emeric Caligari had heard from his colleagues about the old retired headmaster, who lived in a less salubrious quarter of Prague and was constantly seeking work to supplement his meagre pension. He had a reputation for dealing with recalcitrant students, having worked in one of the toughest schools in the city, and was something of a legend, achieving remarkable results. Emeric thought that he seemed an ideal candidate to tutor his difficult son – and moreover, Bruner was relatively cheap and eager.

When Hans Bruner first entered the schoolroom in the Caligari house, Gustav knew at once that they were going to get along. In his mind's eye, he saw the ancient fellow standing before him as a version of the aged magician in Goethe's poem "The Sorcerer's Apprentice". He possessed stooping shoulders, a bowed back and a white straggly beard that came to a point several inches below the chin. He wore a pair of heavy dark spectacles on a curved beak of a nose that gave him the appearance of a weary owl. His coat was long, old and shiny, with wide lapels and a full-skirted swirl of fabric, which gave the impression to Gustav that it was actually a cloak.

It had long been Bruner's belief that in order to engage difficult students in education, they should at first be allowed to choose their own field of study rather than having one imposed upon them, thereby risking rebellion. As a result of this approach, enthusiasm was ignited and a close relationship was gradually formed between pupil and master. Gustav Caligari's choice of subject came swiftly: "The history of magic," he cried, with uncharacteristic animation. As it happened, this was a particular interest of Bruner's. He had written a long paper on the subject as a young man at university. It was always in the murky corners of knowledge that he found most interest and inspiration.

As the years passed, student and master travelled down this dark path of academic enquiry. Gustav's enthusiasm for the subject unleashed Bruner's long-restrained passion for sorcery and within weeks they were reciting the arcane words of several simple occult ceremonies. Bruner's eager student pressed his tutor to move on to the study of rituals and spells that would bring individuals under the power of the magician. This led them to focus on the work of Franz Friedrich Anton Mesmer, the German physician who believed that there is a magnetic force or "fluid" within the universe that influences the health of the human body. Such a force could, in the hands of an expert practitioner, exert a power over the patient.

Gustav sat entranced as Bruner explained the theories behind Mesmer's experiments. "In the early stages of his work," Bruner told his student, "Mesmer had experimented with magnets in an attempt to gain control over his patient, but he later concluded that the same effect could be achieved by passing the hands or some small inanimate object in front of the subject's face. These were later referred to as making 'Mesmeric passes'."

"What would happen then?" asked Gustav, his eyes ablaze with interest.

"These passes would lead the patient into a trance. In this state the patient was able, with the assistance of the physician, to aid his own recovery from whatever ailment he was suffering. A side effect of this trance state was the ability of the doctor to take complete control of his patients, subverting them to his will if he so wished. The practice became known as 'mesmerism' after its creator."

"So... so you could make the patient a slave, obeying your commands?"

Bruner's brow creased. "In essence, yes, but the process was to facilitate the patient's recovery – a process that we now refer to as hypnotism."

Gustav was eager to learn the procedures involved in this strange but powerful practice. The thought of taking control, of being the puppet master of another individual, inflamed his senses. With these skills, he could truly play God.

Emeric Caligari had no notion as to the nature of his son's studies. In truth, he was not much interested, but he was pleased with the effect the tutor was having on the boy. Gustav now seemed more at ease with himself and more biddable; he even exhibited signs of reserved maturity. The boy's father was entirely unaware that this was a conscious act on Gustav's part, to prevent his father from prying into his education and the path it was taking. As well as the daytime lessons, Gustav spent most of his evenings in his room studying the ancient tomes that Bruner had managed to secure for him.

Sometimes, after supper, he would leave the house quietly and stroll about the city in the cool of the night, especially when the moon was full, casting its silver light on the quiet thoroughfares. On these walks he took pleasure in observing the lives of the folk he encountered as they made their way about the streets: scurrying little ants, each with their own concerns, passions and destinies. Drab specks on the face of the universe. He fantasised about taking one of these individuals and enslaving him. Under the yoke of mesmerism the fellow would do his bidding, whatever Gustav wished him to do. *One day*, he thought. *One day*.

On one such nocturnal excursion, he found himself outside a small theatre. The garish poster advertising the show within promised an evening of gothic thrills. The concept was unknown to him but the poster, telling of blood, terror and brutality, was sufficient to lure him inside.

He sat at the back of the tiny auditorium and was immediately entranced by the performance on stage. It was a crude melodrama acted out against a stark and symbolic backdrop, the villain a tall crooked figure draped in a flowing cape with a scarlet lining, visage smeared with green greasepaint. Presented as blend of vampire and black magician, he was the epitome of evil. The climax came when he trapped the nubile heroine in a vaulted cellar. With dramatic gestures, he tore her outer garments from her, revealing flimsy satin underclothes. With a maniacal laugh he stabbed her violently in the chest. Bright red blood gushed and spurted from her, covering her torso in a shiny scarlet hue as she screamed and bellowed in theatrical agony.

The audience, shocked to the core at such a show of violence, sat in silence, open-mouthed with horror. In the darkness, at the back of the theatre, Caligari leaned forward in his seat, entranced, his eyes aglow with enchantment and a broad smile on his pale face.

Chapter Two

With the assistance of Hans Bruner, Gustav Caligari's explorations of the supernatural continued alongside his study of the more mundane academic subjects. As the boy matured, it became ever more apparent to him that in order to progress in the world, to attain a position where he could achieve independence and act unhindered by petty restrictions, he should become well-educated and adept at manipulating events to his own advantage. In order to achieve this, it was necessary to embrace all the subjects in the academic curriculum. He must have knowledge of geography, mathematics, the arts and literature and other disciplines. To his surprise he developed not only a liking but a facility for science, in particular human biology.

As his teenage years progressed Caligari grew more interested in medical studies and saw that his professional career might lie in a sphere rather like that of his father. Gustav took to borrowing a number of his father's textbooks and even persuaded him to allow his son to attend some of his lectures. Nevertheless, Hans

Bruner remained Gustav's real rock and his only confidant. Gustav could never expose his darker thoughts to his father; with Bruner, however, he could be himself. He felt he had no need to hide from his tutor his dark and strange desires. And the sense of security he experienced with the old pedagogue gave the youth confidence and helped foster his ambitions.

Then came the blow. Some months before Gustav was to take his admission examinations to the Prague Medical School, Bruner fell ill. The doctor attending Bruner advised Gustav and his father that it was a fatal illness. "The old man is worn out. There is no way back for him. His major organs are failing. The oil in the lamp has dried up and so the flame will falter and die."

It was the first time in his life that Gustav had felt the emotion of sadness. Somewhat to his surprise, it dawned on him that not merely had he come to rely on the old fellow regarding his studies; he had, too, grown terribly fond of him. The shock of his tutor's illness made Caligari realise that he had come to think of Bruner as a father figure. He certainly had more in common with him than with his own natural parent. They shared a remarkable affinity and understanding that was, in Gustav's eyes, spiritual. He knew that he owed the old man a great deal for opening up that shadowed territory which now consumed much of his interest. The thought of losing Bruner, of there being a world without him, pained Gustav severely. It was a heavy burden pressing down on his soul. He did not, however, harbour false hopes; he accepted the inevitability of the man's death and this made the pain worse.

One dull autumn evening, as the louring grey clouds scudded across the sky, Gustav made his way to see the old man in his cottage in the poor quarter of the city where he lived. As he walked through the shabby, narrow streets, the burden of sadness lay heavy on his shoulders. He was well aware that this was the last time he would see his ailing tutor in the land of the living.

He entered the gloomy, cramped room where Bruner lay on his sick bed, covered with ancient grimy creased linen and a threadbare counterpane. A single candle was the only illumination in this death chamber, as Gustav conceived it. The old man lay on his back, only his head visible above the covers. His visage was wrinkled and grey, like the sheets themselves. The cheeks were sunken and his eyes, dark pinpricks, peered out from hollow caverns.

The sound of the door closing alerted the old man to the presence of a visitor. With infinitesimal speed, he turned his head and gazed in Caligari's direction, but all he saw was a shifting grey shadow.

"Who is it?" he asked, the voice a mere jarring whisper.

"It is I, Gustav," came the reply.

The thin cracked lips trembled into a feeble smile. "You have come to bid me bon voyage on my greatest journey, have you?"

Caligari nodded at first, realising after some moments that a silent response was of no use to a man whose senses were rapidly failing. "Yes," he said at length.

"Are you not jealous, my boy? I am about to discover first hand all the mysteries of death we have read about in those dusty old grimoires and arcane tracts, and to which we could in reality approach no nearer than educated surmise." He paused briefly to draw breath, a process which sounded like the thin wail of a pair of ancient bellows. "As I have intimated on many occasions," he continued, his voice now weaker than ever, "true education is experience. We can learn the pathways from books and have clearer notions of hidden truths through experiments, but to *really* know, one must be part of it. Now, by dying, I shall be part of it. I embrace the darkness." He gave a dry-throated chuckle and then lay still.

At first Caligari thought he had died, but then he observed the gentle rise and fall of Bruner's chest beneath the bedclothes. Some renegade spirit within the old man still refused to let go the feeble threads of life. With a sudden instinctive motion, Gustav leaned forward, placed his hand over the old man's mouth and pressed down. The pinprick eyes flashed in terror and the desiccated carcass stirred in the bed, the arms fluttering like the wings of a dying butterfly. Caligari held fast until the final drops of life were drained out of Hans Bruner's body.

Some little time later, Gustav Caligari emerged into the street. The clouds had parted and the moon shone down brightly. Caligari gazed up at the amber sphere and smiled. It was as though the bright rays were an indication of heavenly approbation. He smiled broadly. It was surely a sign.

Within half an hour he was sitting in a tavern with a glass of burgundy. He raised it to his lips and smiled again before imbibing the warm red liquid. He was celebrating. Today, *I have stepped over the threshold,* he thought. And it felt good. He followed Bruner's precept that to know something fully, to experience the reality, one must be part of it. He raised his glass to toast himself and his achievement. *Today,* he told himself with unrestrained enthusiasm, *I have been part of it: I have taken a life. I have committed my first murder.*

For some considerable time Gustav Caligari repressed his dark desires and murderous inclinations, concentrating instead on his medical studies. He knew that he must master all the principles of medicine and attain a comfortable living as a specialist before he could indulge in his real passion. In a strangely masochistic fashion, he enjoyed denying himself the pleasure of following his homicidal desires. He felt it made him a stronger and more powerful individual. Nevertheless, he continued his researches in hypnotism and methods of mind control, keeping these activities from the learned professors at the medical school.

The same year Caligari completed his studies, his father died, and Gustav inherited a considerable sum of money, which allowed him to set up a medical practice in Prague. He was now a master in the art of dissembling, subjugating his innate desires in order to develop a veneer of charm, ensuring his success as a doctor. Yet he soon grew bored and knew the time was right to kill again. He was hungry for it.

He had been planning to kill for some time, as he considered the prospect of stalking the enveloping blackness of the night-time streets of the theatrical district after hours and taking the life of some random young woman who should know better than to be out alone. An opportunity presented itself closer to home, however, when one such woman stepped, or rather staggered in a shiver of ostrich feathers and fur, into his consulting rooms. Her heavy make-up did not disguise the veins around her nose and cheeks, and the jaundiced eyes bespoke the toll of being a heavy drinker. Her breathing was ragged and within seconds he had guessed that she was suffering from heart failure. She grasped the arm of the chair and sat down with relief.

"It's my chest," she said plaintively. "Haven't been able to get my breath for a couple of weeks. If I don't sing, I starve. I'm an artiste and I need to perform." There was a desperate look in her eyes.

"My dear lady," he said, summoning his most unctuous charm, "and so you shall." *For me*, he thought. After a swift examination to confirm his diagnosis, he prescribed pills. Knowing they would hasten her end rather than postpone the inevitable, he handed her an unmarked plain bottle from his own shelves, thus ensuring that there was no risk of any connection with the pharmacy. On dismissing her, he took her name and address and promised to call on her the next day at home.

Late the following afternoon, under the cloak of dusk, Caligari arrived at a run-down apartment block in the east of the city. He had dismissed his cab two streets away and walked the rest of the distance, swinging his cane, his hat pulled down over his eyes, and carrying his medical bag as insurance against being seen in such an area. Taking the stairs to the second floor, he tapped on the scuffed door of Number 3A. There was no response but the door was unlocked. From the light of a single candle he saw a head thrown back and, as he moved forward, the meagre firelight revealed an assortment of shawls thrown on the floor around the figure of his victim as she lay motionless on a heavily cushioned sofa. Was he too late? Had he missed it? At his step she lowered her head, lungs rasping painfully as she shifted position. He noted the hectic spots on her cheeks and the exposed pale flesh elsewhere, glistening damply in the firelight. He smiled. The pills had done their work efficiently – it was clear that her blood pressure was dramatically raised. She was close to the end. All that was needed was a sudden shock and the woman would leave this earth while he watched. He knelt beside her and felt her pulse. Racing and erratic. Perfect. She stirred as he took her wrist and gave him a weak smile as she recognised him as the doctor.

"Will I sing again?" she croaked, tears forming in her eyes.

"Oh, yes, my dear," he said, moving closer, running his hand across her rapidly rising and falling chest and pressing his powerful fingers to her throat. "Loudly. And for my ears only."

Confusion clouded her face as she stared into his eyes, glittering in the firelight. She screamed once before he pressed down with a tapestried cushion in his other hand, viewing the terror and then the light fading from her eyes as he transported her from this world to the next. It was satisfying beyond measure.

He was admiring his work and wiping his hands when the door flew open and a young woman stepped inside, taking in the picture of the tall stranger and the medical bag on the table. "I heard a noise. I was worried. Is she – oh!" She gasped as she saw the staring eyes, the limp white arm hanging over the sofa. Something about the man in the room unnerved her.

Caligari took a deep breath and edged towards the door. "I am a medical man but I am afraid I could do nothing. A sudden attack…"

"Oh, poor dear," she said. She had been fond of the older woman and gulped back tears. "But what kind of attack? I heard her scream. I thought it was her heart?"

"In the last moments, fear can overtake us all, young lady," he said smoothly, staring at her.

She eyed him with scepticism and he sensed it. Weighing up the situation swiftly, he decided against silencing her. She looked strong and would struggle, possibly alerting other residents. He headed for the door. "I have other patients," he said.

"But aren't you going to make her decent?" she said, gesturing towards the still-open eyes of her friend. "And shouldn't there be a certificate or something? Call yourself a doctor…"

"It will follow," he said, as he escaped the confines of the suddenly oppressive room and broke into the cool air outside. Walking swiftly to the main thoroughfare he hailed a cab, and within half an hour was at home.

Only then did he discover that he had left his medical bag behind on the table of his victim's apartment. The incriminating bottle of pills would still be somewhere in the room; not labelled, but the contents nevertheless potentially damning. Cursing his own stupidity, he debated returning to collect them. He could easily explain away his presence as the woman's physician but somehow he feared the young neighbour's perception of him. He debated the risks for some time but decided that he had no choice. The bag and its contents bore his name, and the longer he left it there unclaimed the odder it would appear.

Within two hours he was back at the apartment. An undertaker's carriage was stationed outside. Clenching his fists, Caligari entered the building. The door was ajar and two undertakers were attending to the body.

"Sir?" said the short, bewhiskered gentleman.

"I am Miss Stein's doctor. I left my medical bag here earlier this evening and only realised when I reached my next patient. Perhaps her neighbour explained? May I?"

The other man, tall and thin, nodded. "Ah, yes. Said she had some sort of attack while you were there. Have you a certificate? Need to have everything in order."

"It's in my bag," Caligari said carefully, moving to the table and scanning the room for a pill bottle anywhere in sight. His grip closed on the handle of his medical bag. Perhaps he could distract them while he searched for the bottle?

"There'll be a post mortem, I expect," said the thin man. "Sudden death and all. The doctor who lives round the corner was called. He couldn't tell what happened. Said she had some marks, like, on her face. Doesn't look right, see?"

Caligari made his decision. The pill bottle was nowhere to be seen. He needed a couple of minutes to search the room. "You might want to check on your carriage before you finish here. There was a young man loitering around it when I arrived – very suspicious-looking. It would be safest if you both go – he may become violent if you challenge him."

The two men stood reluctantly, unwilling to leave their task but conscious of the possibility of their livelihood being damaged or stolen. They headed towards the door, just as the young neighbour entered with a police constable. She failed to see Caligari at first, the undertakers masking her view of the room. He slipped behind the door, but she spotted him easily.

"That's him!" she said to the constable. "He went off real quick, like, without seeing to her properly. He's no doctor." She stared at Caligari; seeing the hatred in his eyes and remembering the scream, she declared, "He must have killed her!"

The constable reached out to block Caligari's exit but he swung past and bolted down the stairs. Without thinking, he leaped into the driver's seat of the undertaker's carriage and whipped up the horses, putting some distance between himself and the accursed apartment. He slowed as he hit a main street, ditched the carriage and then took a cab home, trembling with rage. As he rode, he assessed the situation. He had done badly, acting out of voyeuristic greed and opportunism. He had omitted to plan thoroughly. The pills, no doubt, would be found and analysed. The bottle would contain no material evidence to link him to the crime, but several people would be able to provide a description of his striking appearance, and his own guilty behaviour as much as condemned him to the noose.

Gustav Caligari had to do two things. First, he had to leave Prague within the next twenty-four hours to avoid capture. Fortunately, he had long ago prepared for such an eventuality. A criminal mind always takes precautions. And the second thing made him smile. He would bide his time and on the next occasion he would put a distance between himself and the killings. He would acquire an instrument of death.

Having decided that a complete change of environment was necessary for this next stage of his career, Caligari travelled through Europe and made arrangements to move to London. It was in this dense sprawling city that he would find his victims.

Chapter Three

From the journal of Dr. John H. Watson

In the spring of 1896, I had been feeling out of sorts. My old war wound had been troubling me and so I decided to take a brief holiday away from the grime of London to revive my spirits. After spending four glorious days in the tranquil Surrey countryside, fishing and walking and breathing in the good clean air, I had felt both revitalised and renewed – until, that is, I stepped from the train at Euston Station. The great shifting crowds, the noise of people and machinery, the thunderous cacophony of the place began to overwhelm me after my solitary pastoral holiday; then, on emerging into the gloom of the evening, the thick foggy air of the metropolis seemed to dispel all the freshness from my body. By the time I had battled my way through the throng and eventually secured a cab, I had already begun to feel tired and worn out.

It was not until that moment that I realised how draining city life was. The pace of existence and the close contact with the mass of humanity certainly places pressures on an individual which, it seemed to me, are not present in the blessed countryside. On reaching Baker Street, as I climbed wearily up the stairs to the rooms I shared with Sherlock Holmes, I was conscious that the spring in my step had completely faded away.

I entered our sitting room to find Holmes in his usual chair by the fireside. He turned to me with a bright smile.

"Excellent timing, my dear Watson," he cried enthusiastically. "You come at a crucial moment. What do you make of this?"

Holmes held an object out to me for inspection. It was as though I had slipped out of the room for one brief moment rather than being absent from Baker Street for four days. My friend seemed to have made no note of my holiday. I knew that he certainly would not enquire whether I had had a pleasant time. That was the nature of the concentrated focus of Sherlock Holmes's mind. Such incidentals as a friend's absence held no interest for him.

"Give me a moment," I replied brusquely, dropping my suitcase on the floor with a bang. "If you'll allow me to remove my hat and coat before you interrogate me."

"You know how your observations often help me to illuminate the truth."

"Do they?" I replied, my ill humour still prevailing. At length, somewhat sullenly, I took the object that Holmes was holding out for me: it was a man's brown leather glove.

I turned it over in my hands. "What should I make of it? Is it a clue?"

My friend gave me one of his mischievous grins. "That is for you to decide. Examine it and tell me what conclusions you reach."

"A test," I said sharply.

"Hardly that. Indulge me, eh?"

"Very well," I said. I studied the glove for a couple of minutes, but to my disappointment could discover nothing of note from my examination. I passed it back to my friend with a shrug. "Well, to my eyes there is very little to be gleaned from it. It is a gentleman's glove of fine lamb's leather, so the owner is likely to be comfortably off in order to be in the possession of such an item. It is quite new and of medium size, suggesting that the fellow is of average build. That, I am afraid, is as much as I am able to deduce from it. No doubt you are now going to list a wide range of details that I have missed."

Holmes chuckled. "Tut, tut, don't be petulant, my dear fellow. Not a wide range, I assure you. And indeed your inferences, limited though they may be, are correct. However, I am disappointed that you did not turn the glove inside out for further inspection. The interior of this item is in fact more informative than the exterior." With a deft motion, he exposed the inside of the glove. "Here, for example. Down this side seam you will see some small hieroglyphics." He held it towards me and I observed in small print the legend "S&W R 357".

"What on earth does that mean?" I asked.

"Well, Watson, you were quite right to assume that this is an expensive item to be found only in the possession of a wealthy individual. As such it would have been made by a bespoke glover to the exact measurements of its owner's hand, and these measurements would be kept on record. Now there are only three such establishments in London serving the gentry, one of which is Sawyer and Walters on the Strand. That would explain the 'S & W'. The 'R' would indicate the right hand."

"And the 357?"

"That will be the customer's individual reference number. As I intimated, the dimensions would be kept on file and used for future purchases."

"So you can easily trace the owner of this glove by calling on Sawyer and Walters."

"Indeed."

"What is the significance of the glove? Is it connected with some crime?"

"It is indeed. As you have been out of town, you may not have heard of the theft of Sir Jeffrey Damury's ruby."

I shook my head. I had known nothing but fresh air and rippling waters for the last few days.

"Are you engaged in the case?" I asked.

Holmes nodded. "Indirectly, through the offices of friend Lestrade. Once again he fears that the affair requires a sharper brain than his to disentangle the matter – not that he would admit it outright."

I threw myself down in the chair opposite my friend. "Do put me in the picture. Tell me all about it."

"With pleasure," said Holmes, rubbing his hands together with enthusiasm. "Recounting the details of a case often helps give one a fresh perspective on the matter." He took a few moments to light his pipe before beginning his recital. "At first glance the case seems a simple one, mundane even, but there are complications which raise it above the commonplace. Sir Jeffrey Damury is in the possession of a remarkable ruby... That is to say, he was in possession of it, until it was stolen. The ruby was presented to his father, Sir Basil Damury, by the Caliph of Ranjapur for his services in the region following the Mutiny. It fell into Sir Jeffrey's hands on the death of his father. As in the way of these things, the stone was stored in a safe and rarely seen in public."

Holmes shrugged his shoulders. "What does one do with a precious stone? These glittering trinkets are inevitably the target for the magpie thief and so have to be locked away for safety's sake.

No great benefit can accrue from being the owner of such an item."

"Presumably, it was used as security for the family – insurance against some unforeseen financial tragedy."

Holmes pursed his lips and nodded. "You are no doubt correct in that assumption. It is remarkable how the aristocracy place such reliance on these gewgaws to protect them from penury. But in many respects it is a burden to the owner: constantly having to monitor its security while being unable to do anything with it. How foolish of Sir Jeffrey to harbour the stone in his own house, like a miser who secretes his gold beneath the floorboards, rather than in a bank. Well, now it has been stolen. Thursday last, someone entered Sir Jeffrey's dressing room, opened the safe where the ruby was lodged and took it."

"How did the felon get into the safe?"

My friend gave me a thin smile. "That is the first interesting aspect concerning this case. The thief knew the combination and simply opened the safe. Now, Sir Jeffrey assures the police that he and he alone knew the combination. The waters are muddied even further by a glove, which was found on the floor near the safe. It was this very glove, which, my enquiries at Sawyers and Walters revealed, showed that the owner was in fact none other than Sir Jeffrey Damury."

"Great Scott! So the devil robbed himself! For the insurance money, no doubt."

Holmes gave a beam of satisfaction. "Certainly that is how the matter appears – unless the gentleman is in the habit of discarding his gloves on the floor – and, indeed, the police are on the brink of arresting the fellow for the crime. However, some innate stirrings in Lestrade's brain make him think that this solution is all too obvious, too simple."

"That is unlike Lestrade. He usually settles for the obvious and simple."

"Indeed. Perhaps he grows more cautious with age. However, he is unnerved by the business. He has no idea why, he has no alternative solutions to the mystery, and so he came knocking at my door, hoping that I might shed more light on the matter. And he was quite right to do so. Nevertheless, it does look bad for Sir Jeffrey. Investigations have revealed that he has lost considerable sums on the gaming tables in the last six months and he is in debt for over two thousand pounds."

I gave a low whistle. "That is a considerable amount. I can see how tempting it would be to say that the ruby was stolen, claim the insurance money and then have the ruby cut down into smaller stones to add to his loot."

"Succinctly put, my dear Watson."

"So where are the complications?"

"To begin with, why would Sir Jeffrey state categorically that only he knew the combination of the safe? He is virtually accusing himself with such an assertion. He could so easily have said that the combination was written down and some other nefarious soul had gained access to it. Or that he had confided the details to his wife or another trusted person. But no. He insists he kept the number in his head. He had been the one to set the combination in the first place and only he knew how to open the safe."

"Well, by such a claim he has placed his own head on the block."

"So it would seem. But why would a man be so stupid?"

"Perhaps he is suffering from some sort of brain fever caused by the loss of the ruby, and thus his security? The stress and guilt may have clouded his mind and judgement. It is not unknown. You'll remember the case of poor Percy Phelps?"

"Possibly. But Lestrade assures me that he seems clear-headed and shows no signs of mental distress."

"It baffles me, then."

"There is one simple answer to that conundrum, however."

"And what is that?"

Holmes threw out his arms in a casual gesture. "The man is innocent." My friend paused for a moment and then picked up the glove again. "Then we have this. Exhibit A, if you like. It reveals one other confusing element. Hold it close to your nose and inhale."

"What?"

"Just tell me what you smell."

With some reluctance, I did as I was bid. To my surprise I was conscious of the subtle hint of a delicate, sweet odour of roses.

"It is perfume of some kind," I said.

"Indeed it is. Bravo, Watson. It is a lady's perfume and an expensive one at that, in order for the scent to linger for so long."

"What does it mean?"

"It suggests that a woman has worn this glove, which initially implies that it was she who left it behind at the scene of the crime, either deliberately or by accident."

"Have you any notion who this woman is?"

"The obvious candidate is Lady Sarah, Sir Jeffrey's wife. Surely she would have access to the combination to the safe. There are ways and means a wife can use to extract a husband's secret. I cannot believe she could share the same home and bed as Damury and not by some means be able to obtain the combination."

"But why wear her husband's gloves? They would be too large for her, surely?"

"And leave one behind? To incriminate him, of course."

"Have you any evidence that she would wish to do this?"

Holmes stroked his chin. "The marriage is not a sound one. It would be convenient for Lady Sarah to see her husband carted off to gaol."

"So you believe she left the glove behind in order to point the finger of guilt at her husband."

"That is one possibility, certainly."

I recognised the sardonic note in my friend's voice and the implications that it held. "So, you don't think that this is the case – that the glove is in fact a false clue."

Holmes nodded. "The fact that the perfume was still noticeable suggests to me that the glove was deliberately sprayed to create the impression that it had been worn by a woman. The concentration of fragrance is more noticeable on the outside than on the lining, which would not be the case if the glove had actually been worn by the owner of the perfume."

"If that is so," said I, "the clue is somewhat recherché. Certainly your average Scotland Yarder – and I include our friend Lestrade in this – would hardly be perceptive enough to pick up the smell of a woman's perfume from an examination of the glove. I certainly didn't."

"That is true." Holmes paused for a moment, holding his forefinger pressed against his lips in concentrated thought. "I suspect that Lady Damury was involved in the theft in some way. However, she had a watertight alibi for the night of the robbery and so she could not have actually taken the stone herself..."

"What makes you think that? You mean, then, that she had an accomplice?"

"That is how I read the riddle. I put Wiggins on to the matter. I had him shadow the lady."

"And...?"

"In short, she had a clandestine meeting with a certain good-looking gentleman in one of the small, out-of-the-way restaurants in the Soho area. According to my young Baker Street Irregular they seemed... how shall I phrase this... more than usually intimate."

"Her lover, no doubt," I observed.

"I lack your experience of such amorous adventures, Watson, but nevertheless I reached exactly the same conclusion. Wiggins had the good sense to follow him when the two parted and I have been able to establish his identity. He is Godfrey Forbes, a young lawyer who has a small town house in Kensington. Further enquiries reveal that his legal career is faltering and he is mired in debt. And so a scenario begins to emerge. A bored wife with a young lover who is in need of funds. She aids her lover to steal her husband's precious ruby, implicating him in the theft and thus leaving the ground clear for the lovers to be united."

"It sounds like the plot of a yellow-backed novel."

"I am sure you are correct, although I cannot say that I have ever read one."

"So you believe that the lady provided access to the house and gave this Forbes fellow the combination in order for him to snatch the ruby. She must be infatuated with him."

"But the business grows darker, Watson. This morning I carried out my own reconnaissance on Mr. Godfrey Forbes's premises for a little plan I have in mind. As it so happens, I was pausing on the pavement, taking quite a time to light a cigarette while I took in the details of the property, when the man himself emerged from the front door. I took it upon myself to shadow him. He travelled by cab to Fleet Street, to Thomas Cook the travel agents, in fact. I followed him inside the bustling shop and managed to overhear his transactions with the counter clerk. He was making the final arrangements for his journey to South America. Brazil, to be precise. And, my dear Watson, it was a solo ticket."

"The blackguard. He intends to desert the lady and has implicated her by use of the perfume."

"So it would seem. She is no longer useful to him. He has the stone and he intends to flee, leaving her to face the consequences of her foolishness."

"He must be stopped."

Holmes nodded. "Indeed he must. But it has to be done carefully. Our problem is that only he knows the whereabouts of the Damury ruby. Once he has been apprehended for the crime, he may very well refuse to reveal its whereabouts."

"But if the stone is not found, how can he be arrested? There would be no proof that he was the thief."

"I am sure that Lady Damury, once she is made cognisant of the unscrupulous machinations of her so-called lover and his intention to leave the country without her, would take great pleasure in implicating the scoundrel in the theft. Her part in the affair is bound to come out and no doubt she would wish her deceitful paramour to bear his part of the guilt also. However, I have a plan which may smooth the way considerably and bring about the safe return of the precious gem while also securing the arrest of our larcenous lover. I intend to put it into operation tonight. Are you in the mood for a little adventure after your quiet rural interlude?"

"Indeed, I am."

"Good man. Your assistance will be invaluable. A glass of brandy to fortify us for our evening's exploits and then we shall set forth. I suggest you retrieve your revolver from the top drawer of your bedside cabinet. It is hard to judge the lengths to which a desperate man may go to retain his liberty once it is threatened, and so it is best to be prepared."

Chapter Four

From the journal of Dr. John H. Watson

Some thirty minutes later we were travelling the darkened streets of the metropolis in a hansom. I must admit I was buoyed up with excitement: to be on the trail again with my companion Sherlock Holmes was as good a remedy as any that a few days' rest in the country could supply.

"I assume we are bound for Kensington."

"Indeed we are," replied Holmes with a chuckle, "where we shall be committing a spot of burglary."

I was fully aware that there was little point in enquiring as to Holmes's exact aims in this venture. It was always his way to keep his cards close to his chest until the last minute. Frustrating though this was, I knew I had to accept the fact without complaint.

Having paid the cabby, Holmes led me along a dark lane into a broader thoroughfare of town houses. "This is King Henry's Walk. The third house on the left, the one with the olive green door, is Forbes's dwelling."

It was a bijou residence which, I observed by the dim light of a nearby gas lamp, was showing some signs of neglect. The paint on the door was peeling and several of the windows on the upper floor were without curtains.

"I know the fellow is dining at his club tonight and so he will be late home. We have at least a couple of hours at our leisure," observed my friend with a smile.

Glancing around him to make sure the coast was clear, Sherlock Holmes advanced upon the door while at the same time extracting from his overcoat a small leather wallet. I recognised it as one of Holmes's miniature lock-picking kits. Extracting an implement from the wallet, he applied it to the keyhole. Within less than a minute there was a quiet, satisfying click as the lock's mechanism retracted, allowing Holmes to open the door and usher me in. Holmes then contrived to lock the front door from the inside. It was only now that he confided his plan of action.

Our focus was the sitting room and the one next to it, which obviously served as Forbes's study.

"The ruby will be in one of these rooms, I am convinced of it," said Holmes. "I don't believe that Forbes would conceal it on a higher floor, in case he had to make a quick flight. However, even if I am mistaken, our work here will lead us to the stone. Now, this is what we have to do…"

After carrying out Holmes's instructions, I secreted myself behind the curtains in the study, in such a way that I was afforded a good view of the room. Holmes did the same in the sitting room. Indeed, we had to be very patient, for it was well after midnight before we heard the front door open and the occupant of the house entered. He wandered casually into the sitting room, humming softly under his breath. The humming stopped, however, when he switched on the electric light. The sight that met his eyes caused him to emit a long low moan, followed by a harsh cry of "My God!"

The room looked as though a tornado had ripped through it: drawers had been yanked out of cupboards and cabinets, their contents strewn on the floor, cushions had been removed from chairs and the sofa, pictures had been taken down from the walls, pot plants upturned, rugs pulled aside and an oriental jar lay shattered in pieces. For a moment Godfrey Forbes stood frozen with shock as he surveyed the damage and disruption and then suddenly, with a strange gagging sound, he ran into the study. Here a similar sight met his eyes: books had been ripped from the shelves, papers were scattered over the floor and the desk had been upturned and ransacked.

"The devil!" cried Forbes as he ran to the empty fireplace. Kneeling down on the hearth, he reached up the chimney and seconds later dragged down a black leather bag. With great agitation, he pulled it open and tipped into his hand a bright shiny object.

"Ah, at least they didn't get you," he said grinning, holding up the ruby to the light.

"I am afraid you are wrong. We did." The voice came from Sherlock Holmes, who was standing by the doorway with a revolver in his hand. At the same time, I emerged from behind the curtain.

"What... what the hell is going on here?" stammered Forbes, the colour draining from his face.

"I am Sherlock Holmes and this is my associate, Dr. John Watson. We have come to retrieve Lord Damury's possession and effect a citizen's arrest."

"Arrest? Arrest... for what?"

"Come now, the time for prevarication is over. You hold in your grasp the Ranjapur Ruby, stolen by you from Lord Damury's safe. It is pointless to deny it. There is the evidence, almost burning a hole in your felonious hand."

With a snarl of anger, Forbes threw the bag at Holmes and ran towards him, but my friend fired his revolver, aiming wide of his would-be assailant. However, the violent sound of the gunshot stopped Forbes in his tracks and he fell to his knees in despair.

"Well, well, Mr. Holmes, you certainly live up to the soubriquet the press have given you: the Great Detective."

"My blushes, Inspector," said Holmes with a lazy smile.

A bleary-eyed Lestrade lifted his mug of tea in a toast to my friend. It was some hours after our encounter with Godfrey Forbes and we were ensconced in Lestrade's office at Scotland Yard. The inspector had been roused from his slumber in order to oversee the arrest and incarceration in a cell in the lower reaches of the Yard of a man who had compromised a peer of the realm, before he could be transferred to prison awaiting his trial.

Holmes stretched back in his chair and smiled. "I used a variation of an old *modus operandi* of mine. I knew that if Forbes believed his house had been burgled, the first thing he would do was go to the hiding place to ensure his precious stone was safe. In other words, we let him reveal its secret location to us. It would be unlikely that a body of constables crawling over the property for a week would have lit upon such a cunning hidey-hole."

"Blimey, that's a clever ruse, eh, Dr. Watson?"

I nodded. "You sum the matter up aptly, Inspector," I replied, glancing at Holmes with a smile.

"Well, that brings this case to a very satisfactory conclusion, I suppose," said Lestrade, with a smug, self-satisfied grin. "Although, while Sir Jeffrey will be happy to get the ruby back, he will be less pleased to learn of his wife's adulterous involvement in this affair."

"Indeed," said Holmes solemnly. "I have always believed that large precious stones are the Devil's bait. Few who come into the possession of one ever escape the dark pall of tragedy within that sparkling surface. I wouldn't wish to own such a trinket for all the world."

Just as Lestrade was about to respond there was a loud knocking at the door and a red-faced constable entered.

"Sorry to interrupt, Inspector, but you're needed. There's been a murder."

Lestrade rolled his eyes. "There may have been, my lad, but I am not officially on duty. I'm sure there are other inspectors in the building who can shoulder this particular burden."

"Yes, sir, but…"

"But? What do you mean by 'but'? Didn't you understand me?"

"Yes, sir, but… the murder is connected with your current investigation."

Lestrade now looked confused as well as angry. "Explain yourself, lad."

"It's Lady Damury. She's been murdered… strangled. She's dead."

Chapter Five

A year earlier

"My last tenant was a faith healer. A very nice woman who used the front parlour as her consulting room. I have no doubt that it would be ideal for your purposes." Mrs. Clements smiled encouragingly at the large, swarthy man as she led him into the room. He did not respond; his face remained a blank canvas. "As you can see, it is quite light and airy, although when the heavy velvet curtains are drawn the room can be sealed off in darkness," she continued with forced enthusiasm.

The man gazed around the room without a word. His silence was beginning to make Mrs. Clements feel uncomfortable.

"Show me the other rooms," he said in a slow monotone.

There was a kitchen with a dining space and three bedrooms, one of them situated on the top floor under the eaves. There was also a tiny bathroom with a water closet. Maintaining an incessant commentary, Mrs. Clements pointed out the relevant features of this "very desirable residence" about which she'd had "many enquiries". On the latter point the man did not believe her, and he was only partially convinced as to the former. She was too eager for the "many enquiries" boast to be true. And he was right.

"The rent is eight shillings a week," she announced when the grand tour was over.

"I will give you five," said the man.

She opened her mouth to say something and then hesitated.

"Don't prevaricate, madam. I have other properties to see. Either you accept my offer or you do not. Five shillings or nothing."

Mrs. Clements climbed down from her high horse and nodded weakly. "Very well." And then added, with a spark, "Payment in advance."

The man gave her a steely grin and counted out some coins. "There is a month in advance. I will move in tomorrow."

Within a week, Gustav Caligari had settled into his new quarters. He had arranged the rooms exactly as he wanted them, especially the consulting room, and a brass plaque had been fitted outside: "Gustav Caligari, Dr. Med. – Doctor of Mind Medicine". He had also advertised his services in several papers and periodicals, stating that he could cure all mental aberrations, from insomnia to acute nervous phobias. Within days there had been a trickle of patients, which after a few months became a steady flow. Those who beat a path to his door were, in the main, curious middle-class ladies with too much money and too much time on their hands, but this did not trouble Caligari. They were building his reputation and his financial reserves.

Within six months of taking over the premises, he felt relaxed and happy. He regarded his move to London, his new home, as a complete success. After nine months his medical practice was doing well and, as his celebrity had grown, he had been invited to a number of social events by some of his simpering patients.

In London society, any new fish in the pond was regarded as an intriguing novelty, and Caligari had a remarkable facility for the adoption of a pleasant and amenable demeanour. This ability to be intelligent, witty and personable soon enabled him to take a place in this new world. It was not long before he was invited to several gentlemen's clubs, where he proved to be a fascinating and elegant guest. Slowly but surely he was being embraced by the affluent strata of society, achieving a cloak of eminence which paid well. Now that he had financial security it was time to make his long-held dream a reality.

Chapter Six

In simple dark clothing, Gustav Caligari had made his way down towards the river in Bermondsey. This, he knew, was where many down-and-outs, the flotsam and jetsam of the great city's population, spent the night. Some camped under the bridges, others made warming fires beneath the arches, while the less fortunate had to make do with the stone benches.

As he glided like a ghost amongst these creatures, whom he detested with a passion, they appeared to take no notice of him. He might have been just another toff who had climbed down from his privileged pedestal to observe life in the raw as late-night entertainment, in the same way that so many people visited the asylums under the veil of charity. The poor homeless wretches merely provided a gory tableau for such sensation-seekers. The veterans among the scurvy crew knew that it was useless to appeal to these nocturnal sightseers for help or the odd coin. They were not there for that purpose, but simply to gawp, with the result that some of them found their pockets picked, or worse.

However, voyeurism was not Caligari's reason for visiting these grim surroundings. He had a more practical reason, and his neutral clothing allowed him if not to blend in, then at least not to appear fair game. He was approached by two sad individuals with an eye to violence, but with a swift blow from his stick to one and a glare which froze the other in his tracks, they scampered away into the darkness.

No, Caligari was recruiting.

Many of the derelicts slept in groups. This was of no use to Caligari. He had to pick out a solitary individual with no friends or confederates to observe his departure, or to care about his disappearance. The man he chose must vanish unnoticed and without trace. He wandered for over an hour in the damp and misty atmosphere without success. There appeared to be no suitable candidate in view. Caligari sneered at the wretches huddling together for warmth, trying to convince themselves that they were part of the human race. Those he spotted sleeping on their own were old, wracked with illness and, it seemed to him, in the last stages of their ravaged life – and therefore unsuitable for his purpose.

Downriver he heard the distant melancholy chimes of Big Ben alerting the city that it was one o'clock in the morning. Pulling his collar up against the chill, Caligari gave a sigh of resignation. He was not going to be successful on this occasion. The search would have to go on another night.

In retracing his steps, however, he passed by an abandoned warehouse. From inside he heard a cacophony of angry cries. Like some raucous incantation, they rang out into the stillness of the night. His curiosity getting the better of him, he approached the aperture that had once been a doorway and peered inside the ramshackle structure. The place was illuminated by a small campfire, the erratic flames sending menacing shadows dancing wildly across the mildewed walls. Some little distance from the fire, Caligari observed two figures, two ragged specimens of humanity, struggling with each other in fierce combat. One held an object in his hand, his arm outstretched away from his assailant who was making desperate lunges to grab hold of it. As the men shifted position, growing nearer the fire, Caligari saw that the object was actually a piece of meat. It glistened eerily in the strange amber light. *Great heavens*, he thought, *these two creatures are fighting over food.*

Caligari was held transfixed by this primal scene, the two men alternatively grunting and cursing each other as they circled the campfire as though involved in some weird pugilistic dance. And then the man who held the meat managed to thrust the other to the ground. In an instant, he had snatched up a piece of wood and begun beating his prone opponent with it, still clutching the meat aloft in his other hand.

Caligari took a step forward to intervene but stopped. Why should he? He licked his lips. He would watch this dark and entertaining pantomime to the end. The victim's cries died away and he lay still, but the man kept beating him long after he was dead. It was as though he was releasing all his anger and despair in those ferocious blows. Eventually, he stopped, sank to his knees and started sobbing.

Caligari began clapping his hands as though applauding a seasoned performer. The man gazed up at him, his dirty face streaked with tears. Caligari could see that he was very young, probably only in his early twenties. "Well done. You deserve your food," he said silkily.

"He's dead," grunted the man, appalled at his own actions. "I… I've killed him."

"Never mind. You have your meat."

Instinctively the man looked down at his prize and let it slip from his grasp.

"What is it?" Caligari asked, moving closer still.

"Cat," said the man. "It was mine. I caught it and skinned it. Mine."

"I think I can offer you something better than... cat. Come home with me and I will give you some proper food."

The man got to his feet and raised the piece of wood defensively.

"Now, now, there's no need for that. I mean you no harm," said Caligari. "You are in no danger from me."

Like a frightened rabbit, the man shuffled backwards, staring wide-eyed at the stranger, his expression revealing a mixture of bewilderment and terror.

"What is your name?" asked Caligari softly.

The man blinked furiously. "My name?" he replied slowly, as though he did not quite understand the question.

"Yes, what is your name? Have you forgotten it?"

"No, no. I... I just can't remember the last time I used it. What do you want with me?"

Caligari would answer that question later. For the moment, he persisted. "What is your name?"

The man thought again before replying "It's Robert. Just Robert."

"It is good to meet you, Robert. I am Gustav."

Robert blinked uncomprehendingly at the stranger.

"I want you to come with me, Robert," Caligari continued. "I can offer you shelter and food and some simple occupation. And you should make your escape from here before they discover the body." He inclined his head towards the battered corpse on the ground.

Robert followed his gaze and flinched at the sight. "Why? Why would you do this?" he asked, a note of panic rising in his voice.

"Out of pity. Out of charity. No man should be forced to eat a dead cat for food. It is my small way to serve humanity as all good Christian souls should. Shelter and food. I have enough to share. Think of it, Robert. You will have no further need to sleep out in the cold or go hungry."

Robert's features creased with concern and doubt. "I... I don't know. Why me?"

"I am looking for a strong young man to assist me in my work. Simple tasks for the benefits I mentioned."

Beneath the rags he wore Robert's pale arms were lean but powerful. He had certainly wielded the piece of wood with great strength.

"You may mean me harm."

Caligari flashed one of his encouraging benign smiles. "Of course not. I repeat, you have nothing to fear from me." He withdrew a silver flask from his coat pocket, unscrewed the cap and offered it to the youth. "Here, have a drink of brandy and then we can be on our way. Think of it, my dear fellow. Later tonight you will be sleeping in a warm bed with soft sheets and a deep pillow."

Robert's face brightened at the thought and with trembling hands he stepped forward, tentatively took hold of the flask and drank.

Caligari smiled. The simple action of drinking the brandy clearly indicated that the young fellow was now his. It was as binding as signing a pact. Robert was now his creature, to do with as he wished. At no point could he rebel until he was safely imprisoned in Caligari's lair.

The drug swiftly did its work. In less than a minute the flask slipped from the youth's lifeless fingers and the head lolled as he dropped to the ground, feet away from his bloody victim.

Scooping him up and draping his arm across his shoulders, Caligari enfolded the boy in his cloak and half-carried, half-dragged him out of the building and along the street as though he were a drunken companion. He progressed through the darkened thoroughfares for some little time until he spied a hansom for hire.

"Been in the wars has he, eh?" observed the cabby, somewhat suspiciously.

"Indeed, indeed. My friend fell foul of some footpads. Luckily I was able to scare them off. Now I need to find him some medical attention," replied Caligari as he stowed Robert in the far corner of the cab.

The cabbie shook his head. "He's not the first to fall foul of ruffians round here. Take my advice: stay away from these streets after dark, it ain't safe. Where to, guv'nor?"

Within the hour the youth was lying on the single bed in the room at the top of Caligari's house. It was a room that was to become Robert's for the rest of his short life: his domain and his prison. It had been carefully prepared for the occupant: there were bars on the window and a stout wooden door with the bolt on the outside. It was, to all intents and purposes, a cell.

Robert was still in a comatose state and his captor stood over him, a sheen of perspiration gilding his flushed features from the effort of carrying his captive up to the top floor of his house. Nevertheless he was smiling as he gazed down upon his prize. In the soft glow of the lamp, he was able to see the boy more clearly now. He was a good-looking fellow with attractive, finely chiselled features. He was tall, too – almost six feet in height, Caligari estimated. Leaning forward he examined the youth's hands. They were rough and grubby but substantial, strong and firm with long fingernails – hands just as they should be, just as they had to be.

When Robert regained consciousness, pale daylight was struggling to penetrate the thin curtains at the narrow window.

His head ached, his mind was confused and, as he tried to sit up, a series of minor explosions were set off in his brain. He slumped backwards, his mouth too dry for him to utter more than a feeble groan.

A shadow fell over him and a stranger loomed into view holding a glass of water. "Drink this, Robert. You are very dehydrated. You need plenty of liquid."

The boy needed no further urging. He downed the glass of water in a series of quick, desperate gulps. Caligari replenished the glass from a jug on the dressing table and the boy drank again.

His gaze raced around the room before returning to Caligari. "Who are you? Where am I? What happened to me?"

"Questions, questions, eh? There will be time for answers later, when you are more yourself. For now, some food and further rest and then I will explain all."

Robert, his mind still fogged by the remnants of the drug, lay back on the pillow. He lacked the energy and clarity of mind to question further. Certainly the thought of food excited him. He could not remember when he had last eaten.

After he had satisfied his hunger, he slept, his mind filled with dreams of his past. It was a cyclorama of misery: the orphanage, the cruel beatings, his imprisonment for stealing food, his life on the streets begging and starving. Eventually a deep sleep borne of tiredness temporarily washed away much of the debris of his wretched life.

Chapter Seven

Within two days under Caligari's roof, most of it spent in deep dreamless sleep, Robert's mind had cleared and his strength had returned, along with the chilling awareness that he was a prisoner. The man who visited him, brought him food and emptied his chamber pot was amenable and pleasant, but when he asked him why he was kept locked up in this room, he responded with no more than a bleak enigmatic smile.

Robert knew that he would have to bide his time, wait until the moment was right to break free, to escape. The comfort of a warm bed and plentiful food were glorious luxuries, but to be cooped up within four walls was an anathema to him. It wasn't Christian to keep someone locked up like this. The seed of fear grew within him daily as his mind considered what his strange gaoler really wanted from him.

Caligari allowed Robert's strength to return and provided plentiful food, which the boy devoured readily and without suspicion. And so he was easily able, after a week of confinement, to drug his captive's food. It was a concoction that eased the mind and the body, making both malleable. While Robert was in this semi-conscious state, Caligari dragged the boy from the bed and sat him down on a chair. He slumped in an awkward position like some life-sized rag doll, his eyes open but seeing little. Caligari splashed iced water across Robert's brow to help increase his alertness before producing from his waistcoat pocket a gold watch. Dangling the shiny instrument before the youth's face, gently he made it sway to and fro while he hummed gently. At first Robert simply stared ahead, as though he had failed to notice the watch; then, gradually, he began to focus on the bright object before him, and his eyeballs started to flit from side to side in unison with the swinging watch.

"Pretty little thing, isn't it?" said Caligari in a gentle, mellifluous tone. "Watch it closely, Robert, swaying slowly from left to right, from right to left. Gently moving. Easing your soul. Left, and then right. Follow its movement from left to right. Give yourself up to the bright object. It is there to help you. To look after you."

He repeated these expressions for some five minutes as the young man became entranced by the watch, leaning forward slightly so that his face came closer to the gently swinging object.

"You are now asleep and yet you can hear me and understand all that I say. If this is so, say that you understand."

Robert's lips trembled and his mouth opened, but it was some moments before any sound emerged. When it did, it was faint and strangely ethereal. "I understand," he said.

"Good. That is good, Robert. Now stand up."

Again it was some moments before there came any response to this command, and then, in a stiff mechanical fashion, he obeyed.

"Now walk to the wall by the door," said Caligari, the softness having left his voice, "and beat your fists hard against the wall."

Once more, with slow deliberation, Robert did as he was bidden. No emotion registered on those pale blank features as he hammered his fists in a staccato tattoo.

"That is enough. Now return to the chair."

Once seated, Caligari handed the boy a knife. "I want you to cut the top of the index finger on your left hand until it begins to bleed. You will feel no pain," he said. "Do you understand?"

"Yes. I understand."

"Then do as I say."

Robert pressed the point of the sharp knife and scored a line in the flesh of his finger. Rich red blood began to flow, trickling down his hand. Caligari stepped forward and wrapped a dry cloth around the injured finger after relieving the boy of the knife.

"Hold the cloth in place to stem the blood." Robert did as he was told.

Now Caligari stood over him and placed his hands firmly on his shoulders. "When I say so, I want you to count backwards from ten to one. When you reach one, you will be fully awake again and will remember nothing that has just occurred. It will be wiped from your memory for all time. Do you understand?"

Robert nodded.

Caligari waited a few minutes then removed the cloth from Robert's hand. The blood was already in the process of coagulating and the bleeding had stopped.

"Now," he said firmly, "start counting."

Hesitant at first and then gaining confidence, Robert began to count. As Caligari predicted, by the time he had reached *one*, the glaze of the trance had left his eyes and his body shifted into a more natural posture. He blinked in puzzlement at his captor.

"Have I been asleep?"

Caligari nodded. "For a brief while."

"My hand. There is blood…"

"Just a little accident with a knife."

"A knife?" Robert's eyes widened. "Where did that come from?"

"Never you mind. All is well. The wound is minor."

"When can I leave here? I want my freedom. I thank you for your hospitality but… I am in a prison."

Caligari gave an indulgent smile. "You will come to no harm here. I will see to that. At the moment you are not strong enough to leave and it is not safe for you to be on your own. See how you've cut yourself without realising it. Be patient. Trust me, I know best. I am a doctor. Your mind – it is injured and I will heal it. All will be well in a short time."

"All will be well? What does that mean? How short a time?"

"Be patient, young Robert. Be patient. There is nothing to fear."

Some time later, Caligari sat before the fire in his sitting room, smoking a cigar and pondering. He was pleased with his first experiment. All had gone according to plan. Robert was an excellent subject, so responsive to hypnotic suggestion. And what made him all the more special was that small flame of violence within him. He had the facility to kill with brutal efficiency. That was to the good. That flame needed no fanning.

Caligari had a more dangerous and challenging test before he could move on to the next stage. If it worked well, then he was ready to unleash Robert into the world to carry out his wishes.

* * *

After repeating the knife experiment with slight variations to test that Robert was indeed under his control, four days later he performed a more daring experiment on his prisoner. He now habitually drugged Robert's food so that he was more amenable to being hypnotised, and with the same ease placed him in a trance. Then he went to the door and retrieved from the landing a small sack. He opened it up and brought out a kitten, which mewed and wriggled once it was out in the light. He took it to Robert and held it up before him.

"A present for you, my boy. A sweet little kitten. It is now your little pet. Take it gently and stroke its soft fur."

Robert reached out and took the kitten from Caligari, before beginning to stroke it.

"Enjoy its softness and its warm life beneath your fingers. Is that good?"

Robert turned to his master, his pupils dilated and a concerned frown wrinkling his forehead.

"Yes, you may speak. You may tell me what you feel."

Robert looked puzzled for a moment and then turned his attention back to the kitten wriggling gently in his grasp. "Yes, yes," he muttered, his voice dry and harsh from lack of use. "It is good. I like."

"I am pleased. Your master is pleased," said Caligari, patting Robert on the shoulder.

"Good. Good," repeated the youth, his eyes still focused on the kitten.

Caligari waited a while before offering up his next instruction. "Now, Robert, I have to tell you that this kitten is a diseased wretch and deserves to die. I want you to kill the kitten. Twist its head round until it snaps, until you take the life out of it."

Robert moved awkwardly in his chair, obviously very unsettled by the order. He cast a bewildered look at Caligari, his lips trembling with uncertainty and disturbed emotion.

"Do as I say. Kill the kitten. Break its neck. It is an order. You will obey me."

Robert nodded. "Obey," he said softly, as the word burrowed into his brain. Slowly he lifted the kitten up and placed his right hand over the creature's face. It meowed noisily and struggled, its lower limbs swinging wildly, claws extended. And then with a swift, ferocious turn of his hand, Robert twisted the head of the frightened creature in a clockwise direction. There was a gentle snap as the vertebrae broke. The meowing ceased and the kitten became limp in his hands.

He dropped the lifeless creature to the floor.

"Obey," he muttered and lifted up his hands as though to examine them.

Caligari smiled. "You have done well, Robert. You are a good fellow."

Robert smiled. "Done well," he repeated.

"Now go to your bed, lie down and sleep. When you awake you will remember nothing of what has happened just now."

In his somnambulistic state, Robert moved mechanically to his bed and lay down, sleep overtaking him as soon as his head touched the pillow.

Caligari beamed and even allowed himself a gentle chuckle as he scooped up the dead kitten and left the room, bolting the door on the outside.

As he dined alone that evening, Caligari tried to contain his excitement. He wished to remain scientifically objective about what he had achieved, but he kept returning to the image of Robert twisting the neck of the kitten and the satisfying sound as its neck snapped. It thrilled him and confirmed his triumph. He had created his own puppet who was totally under his control. Robert now had no conscience, no morality; he was merely a vessel, ready to obey Caligari's commands. He would even kill for him.

Kill for him.

One more successful experiment, this time with a live puppy, convinced Gustav Caligari that Robert was ready for the final test. If only old Bruner had been around to share his success. That was his only disappointment in this whole venture. There was no one with whom he could share his great achievement. No friend, no confidant, no fellow explorer of the dark realm into which he was travelling and whose boundaries he was breaking. So be it. That was how things must be. Secrecy was essential. No one must know of his experiments and the power he had achieved over the human mind. Genius was a solitary state.

And so now he had to repeat the tests, with the addition of a new drug he had prepared, to be absolutely certain and to prepare Robert for his first great challenge.

Chapter Eight

C

It was at a society party that Caligari had met the person whom he decided would be his first victim. The woman fascinated him greatly. She was a tall willowy creature with fine, pale, delicate features and entrancing blue eyes. There was an air of sadness about her expression which appealed greatly to Caligari; but when she smiled, which was not often, her whole face radiated not only beauty but a kind of raw passion which stirred his soul. Their encounters were brief and desultory. It was clear to Caligari that the lady took no interest in him whatsoever, yet this actually increased his fascination with her.

At numerous artificial functions, held in the grand houses of the city, he observed her closely. He saw how she quickly detached herself from her pompous husband and flitted like an errant butterfly from group to group. He also saw how she eventually gravitated to a small cluster which included a young dark-haired fellow with handsome but cruel features. The gentleman's large, expressive eyes seemed to reflect his constant amusement with the world. It was clear to Caligari that he and the lady were lovers. They exchanged furtive glances and the way she occasionally stroked the sleeve of the fellow's jacket told him as much.

On one occasion, he caught sight of the couple alone, secreted in a palm-fronded alcove. He could not get near enough to catch their conversation, but from the tone of their voices and their gestures, it was clear to Caligari that their exchange was of a passionate and intimate nature. He became determined to find out more and so he waited until he might catch the lady alone. Towards the end of the evening, she was making her way across the room when he intercepted her.

"May I have a private word?" he said, adopting his most charming manner.

At first she seemed taken aback by his approach. Her innate comportment and decorum overcame her natural instinct to ignore his request. She had encountered the man before and unlike so many ladies in her circle, she did not care for him. It was not merely that he was far from good-looking; there was something sinister about him. His heavy features and a face that seemed always to be damp with perspiration were unpleasant to behold, but it was his eyes, which seemed to hold a fierce cruel fire, that repelled her the most.

"Very well," she replied softly.

Caligari took her arm and led her gently to a quiet corner of the room.

"What is it you wish to say?" asked the lady with some apprehension. What on earth did this strange foreigner want with her?

"As you may know, madam, I am a mind doctor…"

The lady shook her head. "No, I did not know. And I cannot say I know what a mind doctor is."

Caligari gave a gentle smile. "I am not surprised. I am perhaps the only one in the world. I cure human ailments, both physical and mental, by means of neuro-hypnotism. When the body is released from the restraints of wakefulness, it can be manipulated in such a way that whatever traumas are affecting it can be eliminated."

"By hypnotism, you mean mesmerism."

Caligari shook his head. "No, no. That is a fairground trick. This is a medical process which can bring both physical and psychological relief."

"Why are you telling me this?" the lady asked, looking around desperately, keen to escape from the man's company.

"Because I know that you are a troubled woman. You hide your suffering well, but I have gifts that allow me to see beneath the surface of such behaviour. There is pain and distress in your eyes."

At first, this statement chilled her, but swiftly her temper asserted itself. "How dare you make such assumptions, sir? Your approach to me is totally reprehensible."

"You cannot deny that I speak the truth."

"You, sir, are not only talking nonsense but offensive nonsense."

"Come to see me. Come to my surgery. I can relieve your mind."

He offered her one of his cards. She tore it in half and threw it on the floor.

"This interview is at an end," she snapped.

She moved to leave, but he took hold of her sleeve.

"You see, such agitation speaks denial, maybe self-denial. I can ease your burden, I assure you."

"Either you are mad or some kind of charlatan. You are certainly no gentleman. Now take your hands off me, sir, or I shall see to it that you are thrown out into the street." She pulled her arm free and hurried away.

"Self-denial," murmured Caligari, an amused smile touching his lips. "Oh, Lady Damury, you will be so very sorry you rebuffed me so harshly. You are unaware of the great powers I possess." He sniffed the carnation in his lapel and his smile grew broader, while his eyes were hooded with a cold intensity. "But you will, my dear. You will."

The interview with Lady Damury gave Caligari the impetus to advance to the next stage of his plans. It was time to progress. Having bided his time and prepared the path with care and restraint, he was ready to move forward. In order for this to happen he had to secure himself a stooge, a puppet, an instrument. It was then that the pleasure and entertainment could really begin.

Chapter Nine

R obert had now lost all remnants of his previous life and character. He was utterly under the control of Gustav Caligari, possessing no independent thoughts of his own. His brain was permanently wrapped in a fog, which not only blurred his perception of the world but chained him to the whims and desires of Caligari: his master. He was no longer an individual, but a mere appendage of the man who controlled him. He remained comatose for most of the time and when awake he was held in a state of hypnotic trance. So conditioned was he that Caligari had no need to administer drugs before commencing the hypnotic process. It was as though Caligari had removed all the personal workings of the inner man and left only an empty, biddable shell.

A few weeks after the death of the kitten, Caligari took Robert out on to the darkened streets of London. It was the first time Robert had breathed fresh air and experienced the outside world since the night he had first encountered Caligari, but now he was unconscious of the fact. His mind was no longer able to register such things.

Caligari had bought him a new dark suit and overcoat and a large black fedora, and together they walked the misty thoroughfares of the city as the evening made its way towards midnight. Caligari needed the young man to grow used to the environs beyond the confines of his room. He did not want Robert to be distracted by his new environment, and was aware that soon he would have to place great trust in his powers when he sent Robert out on his own.

At length, the pair came upon an elegant row of houses. Caligari stopped outside the entrance to one of these, and automatically Robert followed suit.

"This is the place, Robert," Caligari said softly but very clearly. "Carisbroke House. It is the home of the person I want you to destroy. Look at it. Memorise it. You will come here again."

Robert turned his gaze on the darkened building and gave a gentle nod.

Making sure there were no other pedestrians about, Caligari led his charge down the side of the house to the small garden at the rear. There was a light in one of the upper windows and a distinctive figure was seen passing by the shade. Caligari grinned. *What luck*, he thought. That was obviously Lady Sarah Damury's boudoir, and that shadow was the lady herself.

"See that room, Robert. The lighted window."

"Yes. I see it."

"When you return here on your own, that is the room you must enter. The occupant is a lady. She is to be your victim. Do you understand?"

Robert's brow creased. "Victim."

"Yes. You will silence her. End her life. Twist her head until it snaps – just like the kitten and the puppy. Do you understand?"

Robert's eyes widened and in the moonlight Caligari thought that a smile almost registered on those pale gaunt features. "I understand," came the reply.

Now it was time for Caligari to do some detective work, in order to find out when it was likely that Lady Damury would be at home alone, apart from the servants. He was meticulous in his preparations, for he had no wish to be placed in a similar situation to that which had caused him to leave Prague so abruptly. He watched the house for a few days, noting the various comings and goings. On the second morning he observed her ladyship leave the house with two women; some kind of lady's maid and another servant, no doubt. He followed them and discovered they were on a shopping expedition, visiting several high-class drapers and milliners; they returned with a number of packages, which the younger maid carried behind her mistress like a prancing pet poodle. It was this little creature that would provide him with the information that he needed.

He watched and waited. As dusk fell, his diligence was rewarded and the maid emerged from the house on her own. Caligari grinned and followed her. As she turned down a deserted, poorly lit street, he made his approach.

"Excuse me, miss," he said.

She jumped. "Crikey, you didn't half give me a fright, mister."

Caligari lit a match and held it before his face. "I simply wanted to ask you something. To ask you something. You don't mind if I ask you something, do you?" He spoke softly, mellifluously, while he moved the bright flame of the match from side to side.

The girl found it difficult to speak. She merely nodded her head in response.

He took a step nearer so that she could see his eyes, illuminated by the match. "You are sleepy, are you not? Very sleepy. Tiredness is coming in waves like the sea crashing on the shore. You are very sleepy; you can hardly keep awake. There is no need to keep awake. Let yourself surrender. Your eyelids are heavy. You want to sleep – so go to sleep."

The girl's body relaxed and her eyes fluttered erratically as Caligari's influence took hold.

"That's right. You go to sleep, my dear. Sleep. It is a great comfort. I will see that you are safe." He eased the girl backwards so that her body was resting against a low wall. "You now will answer all that I ask you. Do you understand?"

The girl nodded gently.

"Tell me you understand."

"I understand." The voice was tiny and high-pitched.

"That is good. What is your name?"

"Freda."

"Now, Freda, you work for Lady Damury."

"Yes."

"Are you one of her personal maids?"

"Yes."

"Does she treat you kindly?"

There was a pause. "I suppose so."

"You help her dress for parties and private functions…"

"Yes, I lay out her shoes, while Miss Agatha sorts out her dress and her jewels and so on."

"And you know in advance when she will be going out for the evening."

"I do, 'cause that means I have to be on duty. When she comes back I have to be there to help her disrobe."

"So she is not going out tonight?"

"No, not tonight. But she is having a visitor."

"Who is that?"

There was a flickering hesitation before she replied. "It is her gentleman caller."

"What do you mean by that?"

"I... I am not sure."

"Who is this 'gentleman'?"

"I don't know. I have never seen his face."

"Is he her lover?"

"I... I think so."

"You have never seen his face – but you know who he is, don't you?"

"I think so."

"Tell me his name. I command you."

There was a pause and then the girl spluttered out the name. "Godfrey Forbes."

Caligari could not help himself. He chuckled. So he had been correct. The disdainful lady was involved in an adulterous relationship with that arrogant fellow he had seen in her company at the party, when she had rebuffed his advances. How delicious. It rendered the prospect of her imminent demise all the more pleasurable.

"What time is Forbes due at the Damury household tonight?"

"Midnight. He comes at midnight and lets himself into the house. He has his own key."

"Where is Sir Jeffrey at this time?"

"He stays at his club Tuesdays and Wednesdays."

"So Lady Damury is in the house alone."

"Yes."

Caligari chuckled again. How very well organised it all was. The young amorous scoundrel creeping into to the married woman's boudoir at the dead of night, while the husband was out on the town, engaged in a game of cards or some other shady pursuit. Possibly entertaining a lady himself. It was so sordid and yet so amusing.

He had learned all he needed to know. The girl's usefulness was at an end.

"Count backwards from ten to one," he told her. "When you reach one you will be fully awake and will remember nothing of this encounter."

As she began to count, Caligari stepped away into the shadows, allowing the darkness to envelop him. Within minutes he was hurrying down a well-lit thoroughfare in search of a cab, his senses throbbing with excitement. Above him the full moon glowed brightly in the dark heavens. For Caligari it was a killing moon.

Robert sat on the edge of his bed, his arms resting lank in his lap. His face, with its white skin and dark lips and deep shadowed eye sockets, looked like the mask of a demonic Pierrot. He was dressed in a dark suit and black overcoat. The only signs of life about him were the long fingers, which twitched nervously.

Caligari stood nearby in silent contemplation, admiring his creation. At length he spoke, his voice low but urgent in tone. "You have your instructions, Robert. I have been over them twice. You must follow them to the letter. Make sure the lady is dead before you leave her. Do you understand?"

Robert stood up and faced his master. "I understand," he intoned.

"Good. Then I release you into the night."

Slowly at first, Robert began moving towards the door. Caligari followed him until he was out on the street and watched as his instrument of murder was swallowed up by the misty dark of the night.

Lady Sarah Damury stared at herself in the dressing table mirror. Her expression was grim. *Why*, she wondered, *am I not smiling?* She was, of course, fooling herself by asking the question. She was well aware why there was no joy in her heart. She was embroiled in an illicit, adulterous affair that no longer brought her any pleasure or amusement. In truth, she knew she had begun it merely because she was bored with life – bored with life and with her husband. She had craved excitement, a divertissement that would bring a frisson of intrigue into her existence. She was married to a bore and her days were filled with dull routines involving even duller people. At first, her romance, if that is what one could call it, with Godfrey Forbes had been fun. It added a little piquancy to her humdrum existence. But in time this had become routine and predictable. In truth, her lover had turned out to be as shallow as all the other men in her life. Initially, he had appeared dashing, charming and full of wit, but familiarity had revealed him to be a vain dullard of limited intelligence and dubious morality. It had all been a terrible mistake.

To make matters worse, he had persuaded her to become involved in his theft of her husband's precious ruby, supposedly to fund their escape together for a life in South America. The thought of such a fate now filled her with horror. This foolhardy venture must be stopped now. It was not yet too late to do the right thing, but the matter had to be handled sensitively. At all costs her disastrous liaison must remain a secret, otherwise she stood to lose everything.

She was determined to persuade her lover to return the stone and then they should break off their relationship. However, she realised that she had to keep Godfrey sweet until he agreed to relinquish his hold on the ruby.

And so here she was prettying herself in readiness for one of his midnight visits, which had also taken on the aspect of routine predictability. He would arrive with some small cheap trinket or just a rose, if he was particularly down on his luck that week. They would sip champagne and then disrobe for one brief encounter before he would disappear – until the next time. *Oh, God, does there have to be another "next time"?* she thought. Her mission tonight, however, was to extract a promise from him to return the stone.

Slowly she dabbed her cheeks with powder, hoping to mask her tired features. *Well,* she thought, *I am resigned at least to tonight's visit. Perhaps some champagne before he comes may ease my nerves.*

As she poured herself a glass, she thought she heard a noise downstairs. There was a loud bang and then a crashing sound, as though some glass had been broken. *I pray the idiot is not drunk,* she thought. *Blundering into the house like a common burglar.* She waited a moment, straining her ears for further disturbances, but silence had fallen. She went to the door of her boudoir and opened it, staring out onto the dimly lit corridor to see a darkened shape ascending the staircase in a strange, slow, jerky fashion, rather like a life-size marionette. It took only a second to realise that this was not her lover. This man was much taller and a great deal slimmer. Her hand flew to her mouth as a sudden panic gripped her and she emitted a small cry of fear. The noise alerted the intruder, who had reached the landing. He raised his head, as though scenting the air like an animal seeking its prey, and then slowly he turned towards her.

She caught sight of a pair of wild, flashing eyes and screamed. She was truly terrified now. He stood between her and the servants' staircase so she ran back into her room. In desperation she slammed the door shut, turning the key in the lock. "Oh my God. Oh my God," she muttered to herself over and over again as she scurried towards the shadows at the far end of the room.

She heard the door handle turn and rattle as the intruder attempted to gain entry. There was a pause and then a thunderous noise as the door shook. It was obvious he was trying to break it down. Lady Damury gazed around her, looking for a weapon, something she could defend herself with. It would not be long before the beast without was upon her. She spied a silver paper knife on her dressing table and rushed forward to snatch it up. The door shook again, accompanied by the ominous sound of cracking wood, chilling to her blood.

She gazed, mesmerised by the door. It shuddered with the violent blows as the intruder sought entry. And then suddenly with a sharp crack like a pistol shot, it sprang open, crashing violently against the wall. There, in the doorway, was the man. He was young and dressed all in black. His pale features and dark eyes gave him the appearance of a corpse. He was no desperate violent burglar; did not frighten her in that way. But he did frighten her, as though he were some ghoul who had returned from the grave, for what purpose she dare not contemplate. Her body shook with fear. Could she open a window? There was no time, and she dreaded turning her back on the terrifying apparition. She was tempted to scream for help, but she knew that would be useless. The house was empty tonight, as it always was when her lover came. If only he were here now!

The man remained motionless for a moment, gazing at her with his sable orbs, although she felt as if he saw nothing. Those eyes were dead and yet malevolent. Then he began to move slowly towards her with small, precise footsteps. She thrust the paper knife forward. Before she knew it, he was standing directly in front of her. In the dim light she saw the pale flaky skin and was held mesmerised by those vacant glittering eyes, which seemed to bore into her soul. The fearful vision terrified her so that she was robbed of movement, even of intent. The arm holding the paper knife as a weapon dropped impotently to her side.

With a precise, controlled movement, he grasped her wrist, applying sufficient pressure that she released the knife and it dropped to the floor. With gentle movements he pushed her down on the bed. She emitted the faintest sound, a resigned whimper, as he leaned over her, his hands finding the fine skin of her throat. Briefly, all she saw were those dark, dead, unblinking eyes. Very soon there was no sound and then no light. There was nothing.

Chapter Ten

Constable John Rance reached inside his uniform, extracted a whisky flask and took a generous nip before returning it to its safe resting place. He liked to take a fiery tipple every hour or so when he was on night patrol. It helped to warm him up but, more importantly, it lessened the ennui he felt parading up and down the cold dark streets of his designated patch. Nothing ever happened in this polite and salubrious neighbourhood. All was quiet and boring. *Mind you*, Rance thought, *I wouldn't want anything too dramatic to occur, nothing that would put me to too much trouble or place me in any danger.* However, the odd drunk or vagrant to move on would be welcome, instead of this steady, changeless perambulation of the pavement, waiting to return home to his cosy bed. Still, the whisky helped.

As he was passing Carisbroke House, he happened to glance down the short drive, and what he saw made him stiffen with apprehension. The door of the property was wide open and yet there was no sign of life inside. The house appeared to be in total darkness. Rance was tempted to ignore the anomaly and continue his beat, but the faint spark of duty that flickered in his breast told him he had no choice but to investigate.

Somewhat reluctantly, he unclipped his bull's-eye lantern from his belt and made his way towards the open door. He stood on the threshold of the house for some time, peering into the dark interior, listening intently as he did so for any sound inside. It was possible that the careless butler had forgotten to lock up, but it was possible too that there were burglars inside. Burglars with weapons. He shuddered at the thought and shone the beam of the lantern onto the lock of the door. He gave a sharp intake of breath when he observed that it was badly damaged. There was no doubt a forced entry had been effected.

"My life," he muttered to himself. His immediate inclination was to blow his whistle to summon help, but this might take some time to arrive. In the meantime, the sharp whistle would alert the burglars inside and they would be on him in an instant. With a sinking feeling in his heart, he realised that there was nothing for it but to continue his own investigation as stealthily as possible.

Pulling out his truncheon from his belt, he entered the hallway. Here he stood and listened again, his heart thumping against his ample breast. To his relief, all was quiet. If there had been intruders, it might well be that they had collected their loot and departed. The thought cheered him, and gave him confidence to move further into the house. He had just reached the bottom of the staircase when he heard a noise behind him. Rance gave a gasp of terror as he turned round and saw the dark silhouette of a man in the doorway.

"What the devil!" cried the man angrily as he moved swiftly to the light switch and flooded the hall with bright electric light.

Now utterly confused, Rance raised his truncheon, in order to protect himself rather than as a means of assaulting the stranger.

"Who are you?" he managed to ask in a dry, strangulated manner.

"I am Lord Damury and this is my house. Who the blazes are *you* and what are *you* doing here?"

"Lord Damury? Your house?" Rance stuttered, his mind awhirl. "I was… investigating…"

"Investigating? Investigating what?"

"Your door, sir, it was wide open. I observed it as I was on my beat and so I thought… I thought it was my duty to investigate. The lock appears to have been tampered with."

"I see," said Damury, his anger fading somewhat. "And what did your investigations discover?"

"Nothing as yet, sir. I had only entered the building when you found me here."

"The door was open, you say?"

"Wide open. I thought burglars…"

"Great heavens! My wife is here. I must check on her. See that she is safe."

"I think it would be appropriate that I accompany you in case anything… is amiss."

His lordship nodded. "Very well."

Damury raced up the staircase with Rance in his wake. On reaching the first landing, the policeman observed that one of the doors was ajar, a pale amber glow emanating from the interior. Damury hurried inside, followed by the constable. A single candle on the bedside table illuminated the room with a shifting yellow light. The sight that met their eyes as they entered the room stopped both men in their tracks. They looked in horror at the sprawled figure lying on the bed, head lolling over the edge, eyes staring sightlessly at the ceiling.

Damury uttered a cry of pain and ran to his wife. He bent down by the bed and cradled her in his arms, tears coursing down his cheeks. For some moments he was struck dumb as he came to understand the awful truth of the situation, and then his chest heaved as he gave a great sob of despair. "Oh, God. Oh, God, she's dead. She's dead. She's dead," he muttered faintly, burying his head in his wife's breast.

Crikey, this was murder, thought Rance. The brutal murder of a titled lady. A case too big for a fellow on the beat. This was a job for Scotland Yard.

Chapter Eleven

From the journal of Dr. John H. Watson

By the time we arrived at Lord Damury's town house, tendrils of dawn were marking the sky. Nature, ignorant of man's nefarious doings, promised a fine day. Nevertheless, I was forced to stifle a few yawns as Holmes, Lestrade and I travelled from the Yard to the scene of the crime. It had been a long and busy night, and I for one was ready for my bed.

Holmes, however, seemed as alert as a lion hunting its prey. The investigation of crime was a great stimulant for him. He could go for days with little sleep or sustenance when on a case. It was when there was nothing to challenge his detective skills that lethargy and indolence set in. At such times he was often tempted to reach for the neat morocco case containing his hypodermic needle and the little bottle of cocaine that was a permanent feature of his chemical shelf.

Two uniformed policemen were on guard outside the house when we arrived and we were shown into the drawing room. Here we found Lord Damury, slumped in a chair clutching a glass of brandy, while Constable John Rance, who had discovered the body, stood awkwardly by the fireplace.

"Please accept our sincere condolences, your lordship," said Lestrade in a kindly fashion, after introducing himself. "We will do all we can to apprehend the murderer."

Damury looked up from his drink. "But you can't bring her back, can you? You can't make her alive again." His voice was raw and full of emotion, while his eyes brimmed with angry tears.

Lestrade shook his head. "No, sir. But I assure you that you will feel some consolation when we apprehend the demon who did the deed. And in this matter we have the assistance of Mr. Sherlock Holmes and his associate Dr. John Watson."

Damury shifted his gaze to us. "Sherlock Holmes? The private detective?"

Holmes gave a brief nod. "I do work independently of the official police."

Damury seemed on the brink of saying something, but with an exasperated sigh he thought better of it and took a large gulp of brandy.

"So, Constable Rance, if you could give us your report of how you found the body and any other information that you consider relevant to this investigation," said Lestrade.

Rance stiffened to attention. "Yes, Inspector," he said and recounted the night's events. "It looked to me like the poor woman had been strangled, and the doctor attending confirmed that this was indeed the case."

Lestrade nodded and thought for a moment, allowing the facts to establish themselves in his brain before turning his attention to Lord Damury. "There were no servants in the house this evening, sir?"

"No."

"Isn't that strange?"

"Not really. My wife liked to give all the staff a day to themselves and my manservant, Bowes, also had the night off. That was no discomfort to me as I was at my club. I had intended to spend the night there but changed my mind at the last minute. If… if only I had come home sooner, I might have been able…" He broke off with a trembling sigh and took another drink of brandy.

"What of your wife's personal maid?" asked Holmes after a pause.

"Sarah… Lady Damury had dismissed her maid and the rest of the staff for the evening," Damury replied. "She did this quite often. She liked the solitude and comfort of an empty house. I never thought that such a situation would put her in any danger."

"Have you been able to establish whether any item of value has been taken?" asked Holmes.

Damury shook his head. "No. A cursory glance suggests that nothing is missing. The most valuable item I had in my possession was stolen some weeks ago."

Holmes and Lestrade exchanged glances and my friend gave the briefest shake of the head. Now was not the appropriate time to reveal that the ruby had been recovered, or any of the circumstances surrounding its retrieval.

"Have you any idea who might have done this terrible deed?" asked Lestrade.

"No, of course not," snapped Damury, his voice raw with emotion. "It is obviously the work of some madman. My wife was a kind, generous soul. She did not have an enemy in the world. She was… a lovely woman." He thrust his head in his hands, his whole frame wracked with sobs.

Holmes tapped Lestrade on the arm. "Perhaps Rance can show us the scene of the crime," he said quietly.

Lestrade nodded. "Right you are, Mr. Holmes."

"Either Lord Damury is truly grief stricken, or he is a very good actor," observed the inspector as we made our way upstairs.

"Or he is filled with remorse over what he has done," responded Holmes pithily.

A constable was stationed outside Lady Damury's bedroom. As we approached he stood to attention and gave a brief salute.

We entered the chamber. It was dimly lit and very well appointed. Our eyes were immediately drawn to the body of Lady Damury on the bed. She appeared to be a most beautiful woman, tall and slender with what would have been an elegant face in life. It was now distorted into the rictus of a silent scream, the eyes bulging from their sockets.

As Lestrade and I stood some distance away, Holmes knelt down beside her and began his examination. Taking out his magnifying glass he studied her ladyship's neck, hair and fingers. He then carried out a minute inspection of the room, sometimes kneeling and once lying flat on his face. So engrossed was he in this occupation that he appeared to have forgotten our presence, for he muttered to himself the whole time. Some ten minutes later, his task complete, he returned to our side.

"What have you learned from your study, Mr. Holmes?" asked Lestrade.

"Many minor details that open up avenues for various speculations. It seems very likely that while she was being strangled, Lady Damury offered up no resistance. There is a paper knife on the floor by the bed which appears to have been discarded. If she had meant to wound her attacker, she would still have it in her grasp. Moreover there are no traces of material or skin under the fingernails: there would be if she had tried to defend herself, attempting to force her assailant to desist. Similarly her hair is still neatly coiffured and is hardly disturbed. It as though she simply lay down and allowed herself to be murdered."

"Or that she was drugged," said I.

"Indeed, Watson, that was one possibility that I had considered, but her pupils show no sign of dilation, as there would be if there were drugs in her system. I believe that she was frozen with fear and was unable to offer any resistance to her assailant. He must have proved a terrifying sight."

"Is there anything else you can tell me?" asked Lestrade.

"Very little. The murderer was a tall man of around six feet. He wore square-toed boots and a full-length black woollen overcoat, and had long fingernails."

"And how do you come by all this information?" asked Lestrade, a note of disdain in his voice.

"The height is indicated by his stride. As luck would have it, some mud from the garden had adhered to his feet and left marks on the carpet, which allowed me to make the calculation."

"How do you know the mud was left by the murderer's shoes, and not by Rance or Damury?"

"Because neither man is six feet tall, nor do they wear square-toed boots."

"I see. And the other details?"

"Strands of black wool have been caught on the wooden foot of the bed; no doubt the garment was flapping about as the murderer committed his deed and the coat caught there briefly. If you examine the strangulation marks, you will notice that, above the bruises left by the murderer's fingerprints, there are small wounds in the flesh left by long fingernails."

"Well, that's all well and good, but it really doesn't get us any nearer to identifying the culprit."

"I agree, Lestrade. They are merely details to add to the portrait of the perpetrator. However, all the attributes I have described will apply to the man you eventually arrest and they will help secure a conviction."

"That's as may be, but it seems to me that we have two possible culprits for this crime: Damury himself and Godfrey Forbes, the lover. I don't think we need look very much farther than those two coves," said Lestrade.

"But neither man fits Holmes's description," I said.

"That is by the by, Doctor," sniffed Lestrade.

"Lestrade, may I offer some advice?" said Holmes softly, leaning close to Lestrade's ear.

"You can offer," grinned Lestrade awkwardly.

"You already have one of your suspects in custody, regarding the theft of the ruby. I would suggest you put pressure on him to ascertain his role in the matter, if indeed he had one. In the meantime, invite Lord Damury for an informal chat down at the Yard, say the day after tomorrow at ten, merely to clear up a few details regarding tonight's terrible events. You may learn more in a relaxed conversation than by arresting him now, and allowing him to hire the brightest legal mind to be in attendance when you question him."

Lestrade thought for a moment and stroked his chin. "You could be right, I suppose."

"I am happy to be present at the Yard when you see Damury."

Lestrade's face brightened. "Would you? That may be very useful, Mr. Holmes. Very well then, it is settled. I'll follow your advice for the moment. I'm sure one of these men will slip up at some point and then I'll have him."

"I have said it before," cried Holmes, as we left Carisbroke House in search of a cab to convey us back to Baker Street. "That man is a fool!" His voice resonated with frustration and anger. "As I intimated, the facts are quite clear. Neither Forbes nor Damury is responsible for that poor woman's death, but Lestrade is blind as a mole."

I could only agree with my friend. If the murderer fitted the description as determined by Holmes's examination of the scene, then neither man had performed the cruel deed. It was true that Forbes had a clear motive for killing Lady Damury. In silencing her, he would be able to keep hold of the ruby; but, apart from Holmes's deductions, from what I had seen of the fellow I didn't believe he possessed the nerve for such a drastic action.

"Do you have any notion who might be responsible for the murder?"

Holmes shook his head. "Without a glimmer of a motive, there *is* really nothing to go on. It may well be that there is no motive, and that therefore we have very little chance of catching the culprit."

"No motive?"

"Yes. There are those demented souls in this great city of ours who gain delight in murder simply for pleasure. They derive their enjoyment from the snuffing out of life. They require no other reward than the satisfaction that it brings."

I knew Holmes was correct, but the thought of it made me shudder.

"For example," he continued, "let us suppose the murderer of

Lady Damury harboured an irrational hatred of rich titled ladies, and that is the only reason that she became his victim. Where does the criminal investigator begin in trying to trace such an individual? It is an impossible task. The only facts we have at the moment that could help us are that our murderer is tall and has long fingernails. Minute needles in a dark haystack, I regret to say. If I am right and we have a random killer on our hands, I am afraid that we shall have to wait for other murders to occur before we can collect sufficient information to lead us to the malefactor. I fear this will be a waiting game."

The early morning sun was beaming brightly by the time we arrived back at Baker Street. Somewhat fatigued after our long and eventful night, we both indulged in a hearty breakfast, each of us lost in thought and saying little. After a post prandial pipe Holmes took himself off to bed and stayed there for most of the day. I dozed fitfully.

Lestrade paid us a visit in the evening to confirm details regarding the interview he had arranged with Damury at Scotland Yard the following day. "I am coming round to your state of thinking, Mr. Holmes," he admitted. "Considering the matter again, I don't really think Damury is our man."

Holmes said nothing, but nodded gently.

"In my book, however, once a criminal, always a criminal, and Mr. Godfrey Forbes has already proved himself to be a cunning thief. I believe it is only a few steps farther on the pathway of crime to commit murder – a murder that would be very beneficial to him."

Holmes continued to remain silent, but he cast a disparaging glance in my direction with a gentle roll of the eyes.

"After all," continued Lestrade, "he is the only one in the picture. The only one with a motive."

"That we know of," I interjected, rather more strongly than I intended.

Holmes gave a bleak smile. "You must do as you see fit, Lestrade. I believe there will be another murder within the month carried out using the same *modus operandi.*"

Lestrade chuckled. "What leads you to that rather far-fetched conclusion, Mr. Holmes?"

"I am afraid to say it is built on shifting sand – albeit based on many years of criminal investigation."

"Not one of your solid deductions, then. Well, we shall see, eh?" grinned the policeman, collecting his hat and coat. "In the meantime, I'll expect you at the Yard tomorrow for our interview with Lord Damury."

Holmes gave Lestrade a friendly wave and bid him good night.

I did not attend the interview with Damury, which took place the following morning. I was still somewhat fatigued and, like Holmes, I thought that it was a pointless exercise. Damury did not fit Holmes's description of the murderer and he seemed genuinely distraught over his wife's death.

On his return from Scotland Yard, Holmes gave me a brief account of the interview. "It was a waste of time, Watson, as you may well imagine," he said with a heavy sigh. "Damury turned up with a note signed by two respectable members of his club stating that he had been in their company all evening. One of them shared a cab with him, which dropped him off at his house minutes before he encountered Constable Rance inside the property. Of course, this has now made Lestrade all the more certain that Godfrey Forbes is the culprit. If this blinkered Scotland Yarder is determined to make a fool of himself, so be it. If the matter does come to court, a decent counsel will tear the case to shreds."

"In the meantime, the killer of Lady Damury is out there somewhere," I observed gloomily.

"Quite so, Watson. Out there and ready to kill again."

Chapter Twelve

_ᘒ_

Gustav Caligari read with great pleasure the details in the newspapers of the murder of Lady Damury, his enjoyment initially augmented by the news that the police had arrested a certain Mr. Godfrey Forbes for the crime. He rubbed his hands with glee. *Another life blighted*, he thought. This was a bonus. And then a further thought struck him.

He made his way up to Robert's room and read out from the *Daily Telegraph* the details of the "terrible murder". Robert, who now spent most of his existence in a somnambulistic, comatose state, stared with dark haunted eyes at the bare wall opposite him during Caligari's recitation.

"You know, my friend," said Caligari amiably, as he laid the paper aside, "on reflection I am not so sure that I am happy our handiwork is being attributed to others. After all my planning and your efforts, I believe that we should receive the credit for our remarkable acts. What do you say?"

Robert said nothing. Until primed by his master, words meant nothing to him now. He lived in an intellectual void.

"I knew that you would agree with me, my friend. However, the next time we must leave our signature."

The next time.

The thought occupied Caligari's mind to the exclusion of almost everything else. He still saw his patients, their fees were essential for him, but his practice meant little to him now that he had embarked on his murderous crusade. Nevertheless, he knew he must be cautious and avoid rushing things. The first murder had been so successful thanks to its meticulous planning. It was essential that the same be true of all future ventures, if his great scheme of leaving a trail of strangled corpses across London was to succeed. He salivated at the thought.

Caligari's first task was to choose his next victim. At this early stage in the somnambulist's career, Caligari thought that Robert should not be trusted to tackle a victim who might fight back and have the strength to overpower his assailant. Robert needed more practice first, and therefore a vulnerable female would be more appropriate.

It was a month after the death of Lady Damury that Caligari found a suitable target. He had gone out for the evening, dined at a favourite restaurant and then attended the Savoy Theatre to watch *The Magic Rose*, a new operetta concerning a disfigured flower seller who is granted her wish of eternal beauty by a mysterious stranger who is in fact the devil in disguise. As a result of this trickery, the girl has sold her soul to the master of evil. The plot appealed greatly to Caligari, but of more importance was that he was very much taken by the young actress playing the girl. Consulting his programme, he learned that her name was Ruth Marshall and that this was her first leading role in the West End. Before the final curtain call, Caligari was developing in his mind a dark plot.

After the performance was ended, he made his way to the stage door. Already a small group of admirers waited there to catch a glimpse of the stars of the show. Caligari hung back in the shadows, biding his time. The leading man emerged first, to be greeted by a chorus of *oohs* and *aahs* from the women in the crowd, and programmes were proffered for his signature. Then the chorus trooped out and among them, rather shyly, Ruth Marshall. She appeared a great deal more petite in real life than on stage, and was far prettier.

She chatted briefly to a group of admiring men and signed a few programmes before making her way up to the Strand. Cautiously, Caligari followed her at a distance. Once on the main thoroughfare, still thronged with people at this late hour, she hailed a cab, and Caligari followed suit.

"See that cab ahead," he cried to the driver, "I want you to follow it. There's an extra sovereign for you if you don't lose it."

"Certainly, guv'nor. I can manage that all right," came the hoarse reply.

Caligari smiled and sat back in the cab, enjoying the thrill of this new adventure.

Some time later they reached the environs of Chiswick. By now Caligari was leaning out of the window, keeping his eye on the young woman's vehicle. Suddenly it turned off the main street into a maze of tree-lined avenues, eventually pulling up outside a small semi-detached property. Caligari's driver had the good sense to drive past and halt a hundred yards further along the street.

"What now, guv'nor?" he asked in a forced stage whisper.

"This is where I get out," replied Caligari, passing some coins to the cabby. The man examined his bounty with glee.

"God bless you, sir," he said, before urging his horse onwards.

Keeping to the shadows, Caligari made his way back up the street and was just in time to see the door opened to Ruth Marshall by a tall young man. The two embraced briefly before going inside.

So she has a lover, or a husband, perhaps, thought Caligari as he stared intently at the property. After a short while, the upstairs room over the bay window was illuminated and he observed the young man drawing the curtains. A sneering smile touched Caligari's lips. "Definitely a lover," he muttered to himself. Taking note of the address – 14 St Alban's Avenue – he made his way back to the Chiswick High Road and within minutes was able to engage a cab to take him home. On the journey, he turned over in his mind the matter of Ruth Marshall's demise. There were a number of possible scenarios, but he was determined to fashion one that was both entertaining and safe. The challenge of arranging a murder gave him great satisfaction and delight.

As he sat up in bed later that night with a brandy nightcap, he raised it in a toast: "To Ruth Marshall, the prettiest corpse in the graveyard."

There followed several weeks of what Caligari regarded as "research". To obtain certain information required him to adopt a disguise – a procedure that he abhorred at first, but gradually came to enjoy. Eventually he realised that taking on another persona with the aid of a wig, false whiskers and heavy-rimmed spectacles gave him a great feeling of freedom. He visited the Savoy and, in the guise of a theatrical agent, chatted to the stage door keeper, slipping him a couple of sovereigns to gain information about Ruth Marshall. "Gammy Alf", as the old codger was known because of his twisted leg, was able to inform Caligari that "Miss Marshall lives in diggings in Paddington but I knows she has a young man as an admirer. He turns up sometimes with a bunch of flowers after the show. I think his name is Alan something."

Caligari deduced that this was the fellow she had visited in Chiswick. His next task was to discover more about "Alan Something" and locate the girl's address in Paddington in order to build up a fuller picture of her life – before he arranged for it to be snuffed out.

Some days later, the wig and whiskers came out again, but this time he adopted the persona of a solicitor's clerk making enquiries in St Alban's Avenue about number 14. "I have a client who is very keen to purchase that property," he averred to several of the neighbours. "The owner seems to be out. Could you tell me his name and how I can contact him in order to inform him of the situation and ascertain whether he is prepared to consider selling? My client is prepared to pay a very respectable sum for the dwelling."

It was a flimsy pretence, but it did the trick. The neighbours, particularly the women, gushed forth information about the young, attractive man at number 14. His name was Alan Firbank and he worked as a journalist on the periodical *Science News*. He had lived in the property for less than a year and was regarded as a respectable fellow although, as one elderly lady observed, "I do believe he has lady friends visiting." There was much suggestion in her tone of voice, and in the knowing expression with which this information was delivered. Caligari had difficulty holding back a smirk.

By positioning himself outside the stage door each evening for two weeks he was able to establish a pattern of behaviour. On Thursdays, Fridays and Saturdays, the girl went to Chiswick and spent the night with her lover. The rest of the week she went home to her little nest in Paddington. He followed her there to a shabby little terraced property which she shared with another woman, whom Caligari assumed was also in the theatrical profession.

Now he possessed all the information he needed to construct his plan. He determined that the girl should be murdered at the Chiswick address on the night of the next full moon. The great yellow orb had been so propitious for him that he regarded it as his lucky charm.

To murder Ruth in the little house she shared with her female companion would be too dangerous, too complicated. Besides, it appealed to his sense of the dramatic and tragic that the girl should be found in the house of her lover, who might well be suspected of the murder. Of course, one problem remained: how to lure Mr. Alan Firbank away from the house on the night of the operation, allowing Robert the opportunity to carry out his task. It was essential that Firbank should be absent from the premises when Robert made his entry.

Caligari wrestled with the dilemma for several days. At one point he truly believed he would be unable to solve such a knotty problem and the whole scheme would have to be abandoned – and then the solution came to him.

Chapter Thirteen

From the journal of Dr. John H. Watson

There followed a period of great frustration for my friend. The dramatic events in which he had become involved had provided him with little that might enable him to progress. "One cannot make bricks without clay," he groaned one morning as he shrugged on his overcoat, ready to venture out on some assignment.

"Where are you going?" I asked.

"Looking for clues. Seeking information. Trying to grasp some will o' the wisp which may help me solve this case."

I rose from my chair in an instant. "Then I shall come with you."

He held up his hand in peremptory fashion, halting me in my tracks. "No, no. I am better on my own in this instance. It is at the time of action that I value your services most. Today's must be a solitary venture. To be honest, my friend, I have no great hopes of success, but as things stand one must grasp at the most fragile of straws."

So saying, he left me alone with my dismal thoughts. It was rare indeed to see Holmes so downcast regarding an investigation, and I felt as frustrated as he with not a notion of how to help. I tried to take my mind off the matter by perusing the morning papers but failed. The print blurred before my eyes. In the end I went for a long walk, which led me into St James's Park by the lake, while my mind was filled with myriad thoughts concerning the Damury murder and its ramifications. I reached no satisfactory conclusion, however; indeed, no conclusion at all. Defeated, I returned to Baker Street as the gas lamps were being lit.

Holmes himself returned around nine that evening. As he entered I could tell from his grim expression and the downward slope of his shoulders that his day's adventures had not borne fruit.

"Would you be kind enough to pour me a brandy, old friend," he sighed, slumping into his chair by the fire. "I think I have earned it."

"What have you been up to today?" I asked, doing as he requested.

Taking the brandy glass from me, he gave a dry sardonic chuckle. "You could say that I have adopted the role of a Scotland Yard policeman – indulging in basic detective work. Once again I visited the scene of the crime. This time I was able to examine the grounds of the house in daylight. Sadly I learned nothing new. I also interviewed the servants of the Damury household but they knew of nothing, and servants usually see and hear all. They were quite unable to vouchsafe me any relevant information about the period immediately around their mistress's death, which of course was understandable, as none of them was on the premises when the murder was committed." He paused and took a sip of brandy. "Then I sought out the cabby who was on call in the area on the night of the crime. In talking to him I was able to establish that the murderer did not use a cab to reach Carisbroke House."

"He must have his own carriage, then," I said.

Holmes nodded. "Yes, but that does not get us very far at present. I suppose it is a little nugget of information to store away, which in time may be of use – but at the moment it does not move matters along. I ended my day by talking with two members of Lord Damury's club and a frightful woman from Lady Damury's tea circle. Finally I spent some time studying the newspaper records at the London Library to see whether a similar murder had been committed within the last twelve months. Before I started I was aware that it was likely to prove a pointless search; for, as you know, I keep a very close eye on all reports of murders in the city for my own records, and such a crime would not have escaped my attention."

My friend drained his glass and stared into the fire in our grate. "I fear we have reached a wretched state of affairs," he said at last.

"What is that?"

"We have to wait for our murderer to make some mistake, some blunder, which will throw a light, however feeble, on his identity. One merely hopes that this will not involve the shedding of more blood."

I retired early that night but found that sleep did not come easily to me. My mind was filled with forebodings. As I lay on my back in the early hours, in the darkness I could hear the gentle strains of Holmes's violin floating through the house. I had a mental image of him sitting in the gloom by the dying embers of the fire, easing his mind with a melancholy melody while he searched desperately for a solution to this baffling business.

Chapter Fourteen

Alan Firbank read the article again. It was still a little rough, but that was usual after only the second attempt. By the time he had gone through it for a third time, giving the whole thing a thorough polish, it would be ready to hand in to his editor. But that process would have to wait until tomorrow. His brain was too weary for such a task now and besides, he needed to shave, change and prepare a small cold supper. Ruth would be here within the hour. He must be ready for her.

The thought of Ruth made his heart skip a beat and her face flipped into his mind. Her lovely face. He was happy to accept that he was, as his mother might say, utterly smitten with her. In truth, he felt that he was hardly worthy of her affections. She was a glamorous actress, obviously destined for great things, for fame and fortune and numerous admirers. He reckoned that she would soon grow tired of a commonplace journalist on a lowly publication. However, while he could, he would cherish their relationship and, indeed, think himself fortunate that, at the moment, she seemed perfectly happy with him as her lover.

With some alacrity, he put his article to one side, closed his desk and hurried to the bathroom to shave. He had just finished his ablutions when the doorbell rang. *A visitor at this time of night?* he thought, a frown wrinkling his forehead. He came downstairs and answered the door. There in the half-light stood a large man in a dark coat and a large hat, bewhiskered and wearing heavy-framed spectacles.

"Mr. Firbank?" the fellow croaked in a strange, hoarse manner.

"Yes."

"I have an urgent message for you from a Miss Ruth Marshall."

"From Ruth?" Her name sent his senses racing. "What message?" he asked, twisting his hands in anxiety.

"She says that something unexpected has happened and that she needs your help urgently. She wishes you to go to her house in Paddington as soon as possible."

Firbank ran his fingers through his hair. "What in the devil's name has happened? Is she hurt? Is she ill?"

The man shook his head. "I don't know, sir. I'm only relaying this message as I was asked."

"And who are you? How did you come by the message?"

The man touched his forelock with the index finger of his right hand. "I work at the theatre, sir. It was Mr. Sanders, the producer, that asked me to come to you."

"What about Ruth? Did you see her?"

"I did not, sir."

"I don't understand," said Firbank, shaking his head in frustration, a sense of foreboding growing within him.

"It's best that you do as you are asked, I reckon, if you don't mind me saying so, sir. There's a cab outside waiting to take you to her."

Firbank gazed past the fellow and observed the dark outline of a hansom cab standing in the road.

"I'm sure it can all be sorted out, if you do as she asks."

Firbank realised that he had no option but to comply with the stranger's suggestion. "Very well. I'll get my jacket and overcoat."

Moments later, he reappeared, his overcoat draped over his shoulders. "What about you?" he asked the man.

"Don't worry about me, sir. You go see to your young lady. I'll walk up to the high street and get myself a cab from there. Off you go and the best of luck, sir."

Firbank hesitated an instant, then locked the door and hurried to the cab. The man followed him at a distance and stood quietly while the hansom set off down the darkened street, the horse's hooves clip-clopping eerily on the cobbles. He waited until the cab had disappeared from view before extracting a small silver whistle from his pocket and blowing it. A fine shrill note, almost imperceptible to the human ear, reverberated in the air. After a while a dark shadow emerged from a clump of bushes on the far side of the avenue. Slowly, it made its way towards the man with the whistle.

Caligari smiled. It was all going beautifully to plan. He patted Robert's arm. "Good man," he said softly, as a father might address his son. "Now we must gain entry to the house from the rear. Follow me."

Caligari led Robert down the side of the house. He knew the layout of the property well, having visited it twice during its owner's absence. Passing through a wicket gate, they entered a small garden bathed in a pale ethereal light provided by the full moon. For a moment Caligari stared at his heavenly friend and smiled. It was as though it were a willing confederate in the venture. Then swiftly he made his way towards a French window and with the aid of a small stone broke the pane of glass nearest the interior handle. Slipping his hand through the jagged aperture, he reached inside and turned the key in the lock. He afforded himself another beatific smile before opening the door and entering.

"Come," he called. Robert had been standing some feet away, staring ahead of him and yet barely aware of what was happening. He was in a state of mental repose, waiting for his next instructions. It was only on receiving these, hearing his master's voice, that he began to function with a small degree of consciousness.

"You will wait in the house for the girl to arrive as I described to you," said Caligari sombrely, standing close to Robert. "You do understand, don't you?"

Robert nodded.

"When it is over, leave the house by the same route that you entered. I will be waiting in the shrubbery across the road ready to take you home."

Robert's face twitched at the mention of the word "home". There was a faint, uncertain, unsettling resonance connected with that word. He did not know why, he had no power of reason left, to allow him to understand why "home" made him feel so very sad.

Caligari moved to the French windows and turned once more to his dark puppet. "Be swift, savage and cruel," he said, before fading into the darkness.

Ruth Marshall sat back in the cab and sighed. She was tired and filled with a mix of emotions. After the initial thrill of gaining her first major role in a West End production, she had now begun to feel the strain of performing night after night. So much of the show's success depended on her giving of her best every night, yet she was unused to having to summon up the stamina for such a demanding part. A sense of bored fatigue had set in. She had received good reviews in the press, establishing herself as an actress of note, so why should she go on repeating the role? She had given it all she could and had grown tired of it. The repetition was sapping her strength. She stifled a yawn.

It was, she had to admit, somewhat the same situation with Alan. Her romance with this handsome young fellow had begun only weeks before she had taken on the role of the disfigured girl in *The Magic Rose* but now it, too, had fallen into a routine. They would spend Sunday together, and several nights of the week after her performance, but the initial passion and novelty of the romance were beginning to pall – for her at least. The demands and constraints of their respective careers placed such restrictions on not only the time they spent together but the freedom of what they could do in the time they shared. Alan was, she reasoned ruefully, not quite so exciting, amusing or interesting as she had first imagined. Even their intensely intimate moments had taken on the air of a mechanical procedure.

As she mulled over these thoughts during the journey to Alan's house, she came to the conclusion that it was time to bring down the curtain on the affair. The notion filled her with deep unease. She had no desire to be cruel, but she was also aware that if she did not end their involvement with a clean cut it would drag on in a most unsatisfactory manner. The romance had run its natural course and she needed to finish it and move on with her life. However, she was concerned about how Alan would react to such a situation. He still seemed completely besotted with her and she was reluctant to hurt him more than necessary. She was fond of the fellow, even if not so fond that she desired to carry on in the relationship. However, she realised that breaking the news to him would be difficult, maybe even dangerous. He was such a sensitive soul, and at the back of her mind she harboured the dark thought that, on hearing the news that she no longer wished to see him, he might become jealous, suspecting that there was someone else. He had given her no such signs, but after her previous experience of rejecting a suitor when she was working the music halls, she would need to handle this carefully.

She would simply have to be brave.

To her surprise Alan's house appeared to be entirely in darkness. No light was visible at any window. This was strange, but she was not unduly worried. Perhaps he was about to spring some kind of surprise on her. Her heart sank. She hoped not. It was the last thing she wanted this evening. She walked up the path and noticed that the front door was ajar. It was all rather strange, and she began to feel apprehensive. She walked into the hallway, shutting the door behind her.

She called out Alan's name, the sound of it echoing through the darkened building. There was no reply but she heard a movement emanating from the shadows.

"If this is some kind of game, Alan, I really am too tired tonight to take part. Please put on the lights, there's a dear."

There was no response, but again she sensed a movement near her. Suddenly a hand clamped itself across her mouth and she felt herself dragged backwards into a man's embrace. She realised instantly from the height and shape of her assailant that this was not Alan. He was an intruder and his intention was to hurt her, or worse. The man swung her to face him and attempted to place his hands around her throat. She bit the long fingers of his right hand with great force, like an animal tearing at raw meat. Her attacker sprang back with a muffled cry of pain, releasing his hold on her. She rushed to the door and grabbed the handle, when she felt herself being hauled back into the main body of the hallway.

Once more the man tried to grasp her neck. His fingers latched on to the fine skin, pressing hard against her windpipe, the long nails scoring the flesh. A ferocious feeling of outrage flamed up inside her. She was not about to let this happen. She growled with indignant fury and struggled violently against the attack, her arms flailing wildly. In a grotesque dance, the two staggered about the hallway, Ruth managing alternatively to kick his shins and force his arms apart, keeping him from pressing too tightly on her throat. They crashed into a sideboard near the door to the sitting room and Ruth found the neck of a vase. Raising it in the air, she brought it down on her assailant's head.

The vase splintered into fragments as it hit its target. The man groaned deeply and for a moment he froze, his body becoming rigid; then he staggered backwards before slumping to the ground. Ruth stared in amazement at the figure on the floor. He remained conscious but his eyes flickered wildly and his arms flapped erratically as though he were utterly disorientated. Then, as terror caught up with her again, she quickly stepped over him and ran for the door once more. This time she was able to pull it open and escape. She raced down the path, tears of shock, fear and distress streaming down her face. She ran into the street, ran and ran, she knew not where, her mind clouded with scenes of horror as the attack in the darkened house replayed itself over and over in her terrified mind.

Across the street from Firbank's house, Caligari had witnessed the girl's sudden and dramatic exit. He saw her as she ran wildly down the street and his first instinct was to go after her, to bring her back. But that would be too dangerous. The whole purpose of his deadly game was that he was not to be directly involved. The girl must never see him, even in disguise. There must never be anything that could possibly connect him with the crimes.

No, he told himself, as he emerged from the shrubbery, his main concern now was to find out what had happened in the house and make sure he and Robert were well away from the scene before they were discovered.

He found Robert sitting on the floor of the hallway, shaking his head as though trying to clear his vision. Caligari observed the shattered remains of a vase and the deep cut on Robert's brow. The girl had been too quick and clever for him. A wave of anger swept over Caligari. "Get up," he snarled. "Get up, now!" Robert gazed at his master with glassy eyes but, like an infant who had only recently learned to walk, he managed to scrabble in ungainly fashion to his feet, his body swaying uneasily.

"We must leave this place now. And swiftly. Come," he cried, grabbing hold of Robert's arm and dragging him towards the door.

Ruth kept on running, the fear increasing within her breast. What if this fiend were on her tail, just a few steps away, those long fingernails reaching out ready to close around her throat and squeeze the life out of her – to strangle her to death? As the thought rose in her mind, she emitted a silent scream of torment. Her vision was blurred with tears and she had no idea where she was, her only concern to put the greatest possible distance between herself and the house, and the demon that had attacked her there.

She failed to see the man in front of her, waving his arms to indicate that she should stop. As a result she ran straight into him.

"Whoah there, lady," he said. "What's all this, then?"

She looked up into the face of a moustachioed, red-faced man and screamed. She was not conscious that he was a police constable, someone whose intention was to help her. She merely saw that it was a man – maybe the man who had tried to kill her. She screamed again, loudly this time, and sank to her knees sobbing.

The constable scratched his head. Fifteen years on the force and he'd never encountered anything like this before. She was either very distressed or possibly a lunatic. As the girl writhed and moaned at his feet, he went decisively with the latter diagnosis. Certainly, she was a lunatic.

Chapter Fifteen

From the journal of Dr. John H. Watson

After our conversation following the interview between Inspector Lestrade and Lord Damury, my friend made no further reference to the case apart from observing that more evidence must arise before any meaningful investigation could be carried out. Despite this, I know that Holmes had studied back issues of the press to ascertain whether any similar crimes had occurred in the recent past, as well as interviewing members of the Damury household. But none of these enquiries had borne fruit. And so, there it seemed the matter would rest permanently unless there was some miraculous breakthrough – or, as Holmes suspected, another murder in a similar vein occurred. Certainly there was no news from Lestrade in the few weeks following the death of Lady Damury, apart from the fact that he now had come round to Holmes's opinion and accepted that Godfrey Forbes was not the perpetrator of the crime. It very much appeared that the Damury murder would be filed away in the drawer marked "unsolved".

Indeed, we did not suspect that the case would return to us in such a remarkable and roundabout manner as it did. Neither Holmes nor I realised the connection that would eventually reveal itself between the Damury murder and the arrival of a new client in Baker Street.

This was a young man by the name of Alan Firbank. He appeared on the threshold of our rooms one evening a few weeks later, his appearance dishevelled and distracted. He was, I estimated, not yet thirty, but the emotional strain etched on his features made him look much older.

"You must help me, Mr. Holmes," he cried passionately, taking a few uncertain steps into the room. "I think I am going out of my mind."

"Take a seat, sir, and try and compose yourself," said Holmes in an easy manner. He knew that it was always best to adopt a relaxed demeanour when confronted by a distressed client. His serenity helped calm the distraught individual. "We shall see what we can do, but in order that I have the full, precise details of your dilemma, you must lay the facts before us in a clear and coherent fashion."

The man gave a twisted smile and ran his hand through his hair. "I am sorry. These last few days it seems that I have been asleep and then wakened into a nightmare." He shook his head in despair. "Even that does not make sense. I am... so confused."

"A little brandy may help to calm your nerves. Watson, if you would be so kind."

I furnished our visitor with a glass of brandy, which he devoured in one gulp.

"Now, sir," said Holmes in a firm and business-like manner, "tell us who you are and the nature of your problem. Start at the beginning and pray be precise as to the details."

"My name is Alan Firbank. I am a journalist with the *Science News*. I live in Chiswick, in the house which I inherited from my parents, neither of whom is any longer with us. Some three months ago I became acquainted with a young actress and singer, Miss Ruth Marshall. To be brief, a romance blossomed very quickly between us and we formed an attachment to one another. Shortly after we met, Ruth – Miss Marshall – was offered a leading role in the operetta *The Magic Rose* at the Savoy."

"I have heard that it is most charming," I interjected.

Holmes cast me a censorious glance and gave a little sigh of impatience. "Pray continue," he addressed our client pointedly.

"Miss Marshall would visit me a few nights of the week after the performance and we would dine together. She would never eat before a performance, you understand. Our intimacy grew and everything seemed wonderful, and then…" He paused for a moment to steady his nerves. "It was two nights ago when things fell apart. I was expecting her as usual when the doorbell rang somewhat earlier than I had expected. On answering it I discovered an elderly-looking fellow on my doorstep who claimed that he had a message from Ruth – Miss Marshall. Apparently something was amiss and she required me to go to her home address immediately. There was a hansom waiting in the street ready to take me there."

"Had you seen this man before?"

Firbank shook his head.

"Describe him to me."

The question seemed to give our visitor pause. He narrowed his eyes as though in an attempt to bring an image to his mind. "He was tall, well built, smartly dressed… A black coat with a fur collar and a large black fedora."

"His features?" prompted Holmes.

"Long grey hair which fell across his forehead. A large walrus moustache."

Holmes nodded. "And spectacles, no doubt."

"Why, yes. A very heavy black pair."

"Did he bring with him a note penned by Miss Marshall, or any item that would verify his tale?"

"No, nothing. I realise now that I should have asked for such evidence, but I was so shocked by what he told me, all I could think of was to go to her. I grabbed my coat and set forth in the cab."

"It was, I deduce, a fool's errand."

"Indeed it was, Mr. Holmes. When I reached the house in Paddington where Ruth lodges with another young actress – Miss Blanche Andrews – I discovered that she was not there. Miss Andrews knew nothing about the desperate message that had been delivered to me."

"The disguised man had tricked you," observed Holmes tartly.

"The disguised man?"

"The fellow with all that hair and the dark spectacles designed to conceal his real features. So, what happened next?"

"In my absence, Miss Marshall had arrived at my house and on entering she was attacked. Someone attempted to strangle her." Firbank's voice began to break at this juncture and he struggled to keep his emotions in check. My heart went out to the young man.

"You say 'attempted'. Am I to assume that the assailant failed?"

"Yes. Ruth managed to escape from the fiend's clutches and ran from the house, into the arms of a police constable. By then she was in a highly distressed state, bordering on hysteria."

"Quite understandable, after experiencing such a traumatic attack," I said.

"She was quite unable to explain what had happened or where

she had come from. The details I have laid before you were pieced together later with my help. My darling Ruth remains sedated in the sanatorium, the whole incident apparently erased from her mind. The police are baffled..."

"Of course," said Holmes.

"They have nothing to go on. They have no notion who came to my door with the spurious message and who, one must assume, later attempted to strangle Ruth..."

Holmes gave a brief intake of breath. "It would be a mistake to make such assumptions until one has more data."

"And why? Why would anyone wish to harm her? She is just a kind, innocent girl..."

"There is a darkness in the hearts of some men, Mr. Firbank, which defies logic."

"The police are wandering round in a fog, Mr. Holmes. I believe they are losing heart and impetus in their investigations. Miss Marshall is an orphan. She has no living relative and so I have taken it upon myself to be the guardian of her welfare."

"That is very noble of you," I said.

Firbank shook his head. "I do not see it in that light, Dr. Watson. I have strong feelings for Miss Marshall. I care about her deeply and am desperate to see that she is safe." He turned to my friend, his tone even more emotional. "This case must be solved, Mr. Holmes. The villain must be caught and brought to justice. Until that happens, Miss Marshall will live under a dark shadow. That devil could easily strike again in some unguarded moment... and next time he could be successful in his murderous attempt. I come to you, sir, in the hope that you can help throw some light upon the matter."

"The circumstances concerning the case are indeed unique. Yes, yes, I am happy to throw my hat into the ring. But I must warn you, Mr. Firbank, to keep your expectations in check. I am not a magician. I do not work wonders. I solve crimes only when there are signs that help me guide the way to the truth."

"Bless you, sir. I do have great confidence in your abilities."

"We shall see. The first step is to visit your house: the scene of the crime, as it were. Give me your address and Watson and I will be there tomorrow morning at ten."

Firbank did as he was requested and Holmes scribbled down the address on his shirt cuff.

"Very well," said my friend, rising from his chair. "We shall see you in the morning. Until then I bid you a good night."

After our visitor had departed, Holmes lit his pipe and rubbed his bony hands together with great enthusiasm. "Well, Watson," he announced with a bright gleam in his eyes, "I believe we have a real corker here."

The following morning, Holmes and I travelled to Chiswick and visited Alan Firbank's neat little suburban villa. Having greeted us with an anxious smile, no doubt relieved that Holmes had been true to his word, he led us into the hallway.

"This is where the attack occurred. I've tried to leave things more or less as they were as I kept feeling that the disarray would present some clue, but of course the police have been here and looked around," said Firbank.

"Sadly, that is all too obvious," observed Holmes, dryly picking up a few fragments of an oriental vase from the floor.

"The police assumed that the vase was knocked off the cabinet in the fray."

Holmes whipped out his magnifying glass and examined the

fragments closely. "Not knocked off," he said at length, "but taken and used as a weapon. There are a few human hairs adhering to this piece. What colour is Miss Marshall's hair?"

"She is blonde."

"These are black hairs and therefore belong to her assailant. It would seem that she grabbed the vase to fend off her attacker. The hairs also tell us that he was not the man who came to your door with the false message, for you said that he was grey-haired and if, as I believe, he was wearing a wig, he would have shed artificial fibres."

"Is it possible that he disposed of his disguise before entering the house?" said I.

"For what purpose? It would be a cumbersome and pointless exercise. No, no, I believe that there are two men involved in this affair. A fact which, of course, gives a very different slant on matters."

"Why is that, Mr. Holmes?"

"A random assault, a random attempted murder, may well be the work of a mentally disturbed individual, but for two malefactors to be implicated involves planning and, more importantly, some kind of motive."

Firbank's eyes widened in disbelief. "What kind of motive?"

Holmes shrugged his shoulders. "I could not say at the moment; there is too little data. I presume you have no notion of anyone who might have a grudge against Miss Marshall?"

"None whatsoever. She was the sweetest, kindest –"

"Quite," said Holmes, dropping to his knees and examining the carpet with the aid of his magnifying glass. He muttered to himself and groaned deeply. "Nothing here but the disfiguring bootmarks of the police tramping over anything of significance. I recognise their imprints of old."

Holmes made a further examination at the rear of the house.

"Look here, Watson," he exclaimed, pointing at a broken pane in the French window. "This is where the fellow got in."

"That broken pane is hidden by the curtain inside. I hadn't noticed it," said Firbank. "And I don't think the police did either."

Holmes dropped to his knees and examined the muddy ground for a few minutes.

"Anything?" I asked.

"Simply confirmation."

"Confirmation of what?" asked the young man eagerly.

"There are two separate sets of footprints here. It is clear that two men were involved in effecting an entry into the property, although only one actually carried out the assault. It confirms what I suspected earlier: that there are two men involved in the affair. The attempted murder of Miss Marshall was planned. There is a motive behind this crime, Watson – a motive which, for the moment, is hidden from view."

Holmes's statement hushed us into silence.

He then gave a business-like sigh. "Well, I believe that we have learned all we can here. I now think it would be apposite to visit Miss Marshall to see if we can extract further information concerning her ordeal."

Firbank shook his head. "I am afraid she is unlikely to be of any help to you. In her drugged and confused state she remembers nothing of that night. It's as though she has blotted it from her memory. She will probably be unable to answer any questions you have for her."

Holmes gave a grim smile. "Silence can be very instructive at times," he said.

* * *

Firbank had arranged for Ruth Marshall to be cared for in a small nursing home in Camberwell. He informed us that the minor physical injuries she had incurred during the assault had healed and that it was only her mental distress that lingered. We were accompanied to her room by a Dr. Standish, an elderly medical man of dour demeanour. His stern grey eyes, which peered out from beneath heavily tufted eyebrows, viewed us with great suspicion.

We found the young woman in a pleasant, cosy chamber, sitting up in bed staring blankly into space. Firbank went to her, flung his arms around her and gave her a gentle kiss on the lips. She did not respond. In fact, it appeared as though she was barely conscious of the embrace.

When Holmes moved towards the bed, Standish placed a restraining hand on his arm. "I implore you, Mr. Holmes, be gentle with the young lady. I feel sure that Miss Marshall will come to her right senses in time, provided that she is not disturbed unnecessarily; which, dare I say it, is likely to occur if she is reminded of her ordeal."

Holmes nodded. "Fear not, Dr. Standish, it is not my way to cross a medical man." He cast me a knowing glance before sitting on the edge of the bed. Miss Marshall took no notice of him. Holmes leaned forward and gently examined her neck. Even from where I was standing I could see the dark bruises, the mementoes of her attack. Holmes's expression gave a hint that in studying the marks he had observed something of significance.

"I would like to help you," he said softly. "I would like to find the man who tried to hurt you. Can you help me?"

She gave no response.

"Was the man who did this a tall man? Did you know him?"

Again she remained mute.

"You are wasting your time, Mr. Holmes," said Standish with some impatience. "The girl is not yet in a fit state to respond to your questions – questions which may disturb the balance of her mind."

Holmes ignored the medic and leaned forward, gently placing his hands around the girl's neck. This had an immediate effect upon her. She gasped loudly, her eyes flickering wildly. "He's coming for me," she cried. "He was in the shadows and he's coming for me."

"What is he like?" asked Holmes.

"He is young. Tall. His face is… like a ghost. He has dead eyes." She paused for a moment, her strained expression indicating clearly that she was reliving the experience. "He walks oddly… like a clockwork mechanical toy," she continued, her voice a rasping whisper. "His hands are reaching out for me. His fingers…" She froze, her eyes widening in distress. She gave a little scream and fell back onto the pillows in a swoon.

"That is disgraceful," howled Standish. "You scoundrel, how dare you treat my patient in such a cavalier manner? I must ask you to leave this room immediately. You may have done untold damage."

"I think not, Doctor. I believe that the only way to successfully treat patients suffering such a trauma is to let them face their fears, relive the experience in order that they may expunge it from that dark area of the brain where it has been lodged, causing them grief. In this fashion, they find mental relief and stability. Have you not read Freud on the subject?"

"How dare you, sir! How dare you presume to dictate to me your tinpot medical theories? I am a qualified physician and you are a mere private policeman."

Holmes fixed the man with an icy stare before turning abruptly to me. "Come, Watson. We must do as the gentleman requests."

Somewhat sheepishly, I followed my friend from the room.

I must admit that I was as shocked and dismayed by Holmes's behaviour as Dr. Standish had been. To my mind my friend had acted recklessly and in an insensitive manner, without taking into consideration the effect his treatment of the girl would have upon her. I could tell by the pale and tortured features of Alan Firbank, who left the room with us, that he was equally amazed and bewildered by Holmes's behaviour.

"Really, Mr. Holmes, was that absolutely necessary?" he managed to stammer with indignation as we reached the bottom of the staircase.

Holmes gave him an indulgent smile. "I believe it was, and trust me, no real harm has been done to Miss Marshall. I predict that in a couple of days she will be well on the way to being her natural self again. Now she has come to terms with what happened to her, faced her demons as it were, I am sure that all she requires is further rest and comfort and she will emerge from the dark cell where she currently resides. And, I have to say, my visit here has been most instructive."

"In what way?" asked Firbank.

"I prefer not to divulge any information I have gleaned at present. I need to build up a more complete picture before I can deal with certainties and various scenarios. Suffice it to say that I have collected a few crumbs today."

"You are going to continue with the case."

Holmes nodded with a smile. "Yes, Mr. Firbank. I would not miss it for the world."

I was silent on our trip back to Baker Street, and it was only when we reached our sitting room that Holmes tackled me concerning my demeanour.

"You are angry with me, aren't you, Watson? Angry at the way I treated the young woman."

"Yes. Yes, I am. You behaved in an uncaring and brutal fashion in order to achieve your own ends without considering for one moment the delicacy of Miss Marshall's condition."

Holmes threw his arms up in the air. "You are right, of course, Watson. In such circumstances I cannot help myself. I always place my investigation first before considering the effect my actions have on others. It is a weakness and a strength, I suppose."

"It is selfish and cruel," I snapped. "And then you added insult to injury by spouting some kind of medical gobbledygook about the experience being cathartic and stating some nonsense about Freud in support of your outrageous behaviour."

"I stand well and truly chastised," sighed Holmes, dropping into his chair. "Please accept my apologies."

"It is not I to whom you should apologise but to the old doctor, to our client, and most of all to Miss Marshall herself."

"I don't think I wish to go as far as that. My behaviour was perhaps a little rash but it did bear fruit. In the end, that will benefit both the young woman and our client. Perhaps now we may return to our normal civilities?"

I let out an inarticulate growl and snatched up the newspaper. I realised now that my anger had transformed itself into petulance and words failed me. I tried to read but the print swam before my eyes, and so after a while I cast the rag aside.

"Why not have a pipe, old fellow. It will put you in a better humour."

I opened my mouth to utter a stinging rebuff, but instead I did as Holmes suggested. As I sat back in my chair, my ship's tobacco having a soothing effect on my shredded nerves, one phrase that

Holmes had used nagged at me and refused to leave my thoughts. In the end, I could not resist airing my curiosity.

"What did you mean that your visit to Miss Marshall today 'bore fruit'?" I asked in a calm, matter-of-fact manner.

Holmes flashed me a warm smile. "I wondered how long it would be before you asked me that. Well, first of all, there were the remnants of the wound at the girl's neck. I had seen those identical marks before. The same spacing of the spatulate fingers and, more importantly, the indentations in the flesh made by the long fingernails of the assailant. They were an exact replica of the marks left on Lady Damury's throat."

"What!" I cried, sitting bolt upright in the chair.

"Indeed, they were identical. I am convinced they were made by the same man."

"That is incredible."

"Remarkable but not incredible. Also, the girl told us he was tall, a fact that I established by studying the footprints left in Lady Damury's boudoir. Miss Marshall also said a strange thing: that her attacker walked like a mechanical man. What does that suggest to you?"

I paused for a moment and considered the question. "Could it be that he had some kind of physical disability... or perhaps that he was in some kind of trance?"

Holmes beamed. "The latter scenario appeals to me. If the fellow was 'in some kind of trance', this suggests that he was not fully in control of his own actions. Certainly, Miss Marshall managed to foil his attempts by hitting him with a vase. Surely a savage murderer would not be put off by such mild violence. She did not knock him unconscious or he would have been discovered by the police. It would seem that this blow interfered with his intentions and broke his concentration."

I felt a chill run down my spine. "Holmes, what are you saying?" I asked, although the answer was already hovering in the darkness of my mind.

"I am saying nothing precisely, merely playing with ideas. It seems to me, however, entirely possible that our assailant is the puppet of the man with the fake hair and the big moustache who turned up on Firbank's doorstep. Perhaps in some way this fellow is able to manipulate the murderer to carry out his intentions. Remember the young woman's reference to his dead eyes, as though he were unconscious of what he was doing."

"As though he were hypnotised!" I exclaimed. "I have just been reading in *The Lancet* about a series of experiments based on the early work of James Braid, who is regarded by many as the first exponent of the practice of hypnotherapy in his medical work. It was penned by Professor Christopher Clark, who has been carrying out a series of experiments to see how hypnotism might allow invasive surgery without the use of anaesthetics. Clark suggests that under deep hypnosis, the patient can be controlled utterly, to the extent that he can be commanded to ignore pain."

Holmes's eyes lit up. "Fascinating," he said with some excitement. "In other words, when the patient is under the full influence of the hypnotist, he is completely in his power. And if the hypnotist is of evil intent, there is no knowing what he can persuade the patient to do."

"That is a horrible prospect."

"Indeed, Watson, we might easily move into the realm of murder by proxy. I have a little knowledge of the subject myself, but I would very much like to peruse that article in *The Lancet*. It may help me clarify some concerns and considerations which are beginning to form in my brain."

I retrieved the magazine from the bookshelf and passed it to my friend, who read the article with great interest. I waited in anticipation for his response.

"Most interesting," he said at length, casting the copy aside. "In lieu of any other avenues of investigation at present, it may serve us well to pursue this one. I think a visit to Professor Christopher Clark would prove most enlightening."

Chapter Sixteen

"And when I snap my fingers, you will return to full consciousness." Caligari waved his hand before his patient and clicked his fingers. Enid Beaumont stirred on the couch. At first her eyes flickered erratically and then they opened wide in dreamy wonderment. She sat up and stared into the face of Gustav Caligari, which quickly came into focus.

"Oh," said Mrs. Beaumont, with some surprise. "Did it work? Did I go to sleep?"

"Indeed you did, dear lady. I believe the session has been most successful. I made suggestions to your unconscious self which are now firmly lodged in your mind. No longer will you exhibit fear of any feline that you happen to encounter. That irrationality is now a thing of the past."

"Oh, my goodness, how wonderful," she gushed. "You are a miracle worker, Dr. Caligari. I don't know how to thank you."

"Thanks are unnecessary. The payment of my fee is sufficient reward."

"Ah, yes, of course." Mrs. Beaumont reached inside her reticule and produced a number of notes, which she passed to Caligari. "That is correct, isn't it?"

Caligari counted the notes and nodded. "Indeed it is."

His patient rose from the couch and shook his hand vigorously. "Thank you so much. I cannot tell you how you have brought so much peace to my mind."

Caligari gave her an indulgent smile and ushered her out of the room. When she had gone, he dropped down into the chair behind his desk with a heavy sigh. He was so bored with ministering to these pathetic women with their tiresome foibles. The process of dealing with them was tedious in the extreme, but the fees they paid were essential to maintain his lifestyle. However, he realised that if he was honest with himself, the parade of weak-willed, needy clients he was forced to deal was not the cause of his misery and despondency; it was the failure of his last exploit with Robert. He had planned things meticulously only to be let down in the final moments. He might easily blame Robert for the failure, but in his heart he knew that it was himself who was at fault. He had omitted to prime his puppet for the eventuality that the victim would fight back. He had failed to instil into Robert's psyche the rapacious, vicious killer instinct that would overcome such resistance. It was there, of course. He remembered the attack that Robert had launched upon the man who tried to steal his meat – the frenzy of the blows he rained down on him. However, the fact that Robert had been prevented so easily from killing the Marshall girl had undermined Caligari's confidence and had brought a pause, if not a halt, to future plans. Could he reawaken Robert's ferocity in order to ensure that he would carry out the next killing without fail? Or was that beyond his capabilities?

The more he mulled the situation over, the more confused and uncertain he became. Then a thought struck him, one that he realised should have occurred to him straight away. Perhaps, he now pondered, the sense of failure he was experiencing could be eradicated if a further, successful attempt were made on Ruth Marshall. As the thought settled in his mind, Caligari felt a lightening of the spirits. The notion heartened him. It certainly was a plan worth pursuing. He would have to discover where the girl was now, and then he would have to work hard with Robert in order to prepare him for the new mission. But these were challenges that he was more than ready to undertake.

He chuckled to himself. *This is indeed the way forward,* he thought with great enthusiasm, his eyes alight with a dark malignant fire.

Chapter Seventeen

From the journal of Dr. John H. Watson

Professor Christopher Clark carried out his psychiatric researches at St Mary Bethlehem Hospital, St George's Fields. It was commonly known to Londoners as Bedlam, and had an infamous history of cruelty and barbarity in the treatment of its mentally disturbed inmates. I had on one occasion visited the establishment in my early days of medical training, and the experience was branded firmly on my memory. It is true to say that it was no longer the inhumane house of horror it had been in the distant past, but nevertheless I had left the building with a feeling of great sadness and sympathy for the poor souls incarcerated therein, and a fierce indignation at the brusque and harsh treatment they received at the hands of their supposed carers.

Holmes had contacted Professor Clark expressing a wish to discuss his article in *The Lancet*. The professor had replied promptly, inviting us to his research laboratory at the hospital. I viewed a return visit to the place with a certain degree of apprehension. I knew that we would have no reason to come in contact with the wards, but nevertheless the whole place exuded an air of misery and despair that somehow infected the soul. I am not an over-sensitive man when it comes to medical matters; as a doctor, one has to build a protective shell around one's feelings in order to do the job properly. But what affected me always was the cavalier and sometimes openly cruel ways in which certain medical personnel treated those patients with mental traumas.

On arriving at the hospital, we announced our presence at the main desk and an orderly was dispatched to take us to Professor Clark's laboratory. As we made our way up the wide, winding staircase, the air was filled with the sound of the patients' muted cries and groans. I glanced at Holmes, and his stern features and pursed lips told me that he was experiencing the same feelings of sadness and unease as I. It was with some relief that we reached the door of the lab. The orderly knocked loudly, entered and introduced us before making a swift exit.

Professor Christopher Clark, a man in his sixties, was short in height, but very bulky of body and in possession of a full grey beard, which in some way compensated for the loss of most of the hair on the top of his head. Two bright blue eyes peered out at us from behind a pair of gold spectacles and his rosy-coloured nose gave evidence that he was a regular imbiber.

He stepped towards us with a broad grin on his face, took hold of my friend's hand and shook it vigorously. "Mr. Holmes, how delightful to meet you. I have, of course, read much about your work. I find your methods of investigating crime absolutely fascinating. And you, sir," he said turning to me, "must be the equally celebrated Dr. Watson." He grabbed my hand and repeated the animated shaking.

"We appreciate that you have found the time to see us," Holmes said.

"I must admit, when I received your telegram I was most intrigued and somewhat puzzled as to how on earth I could help you."

"I am interested in your work in the field of hypnotism."

Professor Clark's face lit up. "Ah, yes. Hypnotism is a great passion of mine. I do believe it is one of the greatest boons to medical science. We have some way to go before methods are perfected, but already I am able to use it on the patients here with remarkable success."

"In what way?"

"In several ways. So many of the patients – I insist on referring to them as patients rather than the crude term 'inmates' used by the orderlies and superintendents – so many of the patients suffer from an extreme anxiety complex. Through hypnotism it is possible to ease their troubled minds somewhat. Not to cure them, you understand, but to help regulate their behaviour to a degree. A tortured mind will always act without reason or rationale. If we can ease that torture – diminish its flame, as it were – we can reduce the patient's unpredictability."

"The regulation of behaviour interests me greatly," said my friend earnestly. "In particular I wish to learn just how much control you are able to exert over an individual."

The professor pursed his lips and touched his chin with his right index finger. "Ah, well, that is difficult to say. To a large extent it depends on the individual. The poor devils who live here have minds which are diseased, to a greater or lesser degree, and therefore are more susceptible to suggestion and control than, say, the man in the street, who may well make a conscious, determined effort to resist the hypnotic process. Each individual has a different level of resistance. For example, I very much doubt that I could place you in a hypnotic trance. You have a strong independent mind, which I am sure I would fail to master. But weak minds... that is another matter."

"And unsuspecting minds? Is it possible to hypnotise a subject if he is not fully aware that you are doing so?"

The professor thought for a moment. "Yes, I suppose so, if the conditions were favourable for such an operation. However, here in this hospital there is no need for such subterfuge."

"When an individual is in a hypnotic trance, to what extent can you take control of his actions? Is it possible to make your subject behave contrary to his own nature?"

"To act against his will, you mean?"

Holmes nodded.

"Yes, it is possible to some extent. We all have within us dark elements that a skilled hypnotist may well be able to tap into. The hypnotised person appears to heed only the communications of the hypnotist and typically responds in an uncritical, automatic fashion to his instruction, while ignoring all other aspects of the environment. In a hypnotic state an individual tends to see, feel, smell, and otherwise perceive in accordance with the hypnotist's suggestions, even though these may be in apparent contradiction to the stimuli actually present in that environment. The effects of hypnosis are not limited to sensory change, you understand; even the subject's memory and awareness of self may be altered by suggestion. It is also the case that the effects of ideas, notions and, indeed, instructions presented by the hypnotist may be extended post-hypnotically into the subject's subsequent waking activity. You may make a person forget what he has done while in a trance, or indeed, believe he has done something he has not."

"Is it possible to instruct a hypnotised person to kill?"

Clark's eyes widened in surprise. "My goodness, Mr. Holmes,

that is a question!" he said, with some degree of warmth.

"And the answer?"

"The answer is not a simple one. It certainly is possible if the subject has within him an inherent violent nature, one that can be enhanced by hypnotic suggestion. I very much doubt you could persuade a loving mother or a virtuous member of the clergy to commit such a crime, for example, but certainly you may have more success with a criminal lowlife or an individual who has successfully hidden a predisposition to violence." He paused and thought for a moment before continuing. "There is one other possibility."

"Yes," Holmes responded softly.

"I have no evidence to support what I am about to suggest. It is not an area of research that I have dealt with, but it seems to me that it may be possible for a very skilled hypnotist to create the kind of aggression required to kill in the mind of his subject, perhaps by planting a false idea that he is under extreme threat, to foster this urge to destroy while eliminating all moral barriers to committing such an act." The professor shrugged his shoulders. "It is only an idea, not even a theory."

"But very interesting none the less," observed my friend with a tight smile.

"Mr. Holmes, may I ask what particular interest in hypnotism brings you here?"

Holmes paused for a moment. I knew that he was reluctant to reveal the details of his enquiry, but at the same time it was necessary to provide some convincing answer for the professor.

"I am in the early stages of an investigation where it is possible that hypnotism has been used," he said at length. "It is by no means certain, but I am aware my knowledge of the subject is sketchy and I wished to learn more. That is all I feel I can convey to you at this moment. The situation is rather delicate."

"I see." There was more pursing of lips before our host continued. "In that case, perhaps you would care to witness a demonstration. A practical experience is worth a raft of words."

"That would be most interesting," agreed Holmes with enthusiasm.

"Come, then, let us go down to the cells and visit a patient of mine who is particularly susceptible to the powers of hypnotism."

Without further discussion, Professor Clark led us to the rear of the lab, through a door and down a shadowy spiral stone staircase to the lower reaches of the hospital. At the bottom we reached a large antechamber, illuminated by flickering gaslight which sent eerie ill-formed shapes skittering across the damp stone walls. It was here that we encountered a burly, black-bearded, uniformed individual, seated by a large metal door. I assumed that he was a guard, keeping watch over the patients. He stood up as we approached.

"Ah, Jenkins, I have two important visitors with me and I should like to look in on Margaret," said the professor.

"Very well, sir," came the muted reply. The fellow unhooked a large ring of keys from his belt and opened the metal door. Beyond I could see a narrow corridor with a series of doors on either side. Odd, subhuman noises could be heard emanating from some of them: souls in torment, I assumed, each one trapped in his or her own little cell with only their doomed and twisted thoughts to keep them company. It struck me that to be incarcerated in such a fashion was enough to send even the sanest fellow mad. I shuddered at the thought of their terrible plight. Leading the way, the guard moved along to the third door and gazed through the small barred aperture.

"Visitors for you, Margaret," he growled through the bars and then unlocked the door.

We entered what was, in essence, a prison cell. It was little different from the chambers I had seen when visiting various police stations with Holmes. There was a chair, a narrow bed with a straw mattress, and a small table on which stood a water jug and bowl. The room was illuminated by a ceiling lantern which cast over the surroundings a muddy and frail yellow light. In truth, I was horrified that such a place was to be found in a building that bore the name "hospital".

The occupant of the room sat hunched on the bed, her back towards us. Professor Clark approached her and placed his hand gently on her shoulder. She flinched momentarily, curling in on herself.

"Hello, Margaret," he said. "It's Professor Clark. I've brought two of my friends to see you."

Very slowly, she turned to face us. It was a gaunt and haunted visage that stared in our direction. The dry, flaky skin was alabaster white, the dark eyes sunken deep into the skull, the thin cracked lips pulled back in a weird rictus smile, exposing an irregular row of brown teeth. Her face was wreathed by a curtain of wild, straggly white hair. I was unable to determine the sad creature's age, but I suspected that she was much younger than suggested by her haggard appearance. I wondered what circumstances had brought her to this dreadful state.

"Hello, Professor," she said faintly, her lips hardly moving.

"I've come to give you another of your little dreams. Those little dreams that make you feel better."

The woman nodded. There was no emotion evident in the action.

"You like those, don't you?"

She nodded again and this time her lips trembled with a thin smile. "I like feeling better," she said.

The professor gave us a knowing look before pulling up the chair and sitting opposite his patient. He withdrew from his waistcoat a silver pocket watch and dangled it in front of the woman. It twinkled brightly in the guttering candlelight.

"You know what to do, Margaret. Follow the watch with your eyes. See how it swings to and fro. To and fro like a lovely shiny pendulum."

She leaned forward and did as she was bid, her eyes fixed rigidly on the watch. Soon her head was rocking gently in rhythm with its swaying movement.

"You are beginning to feel sleepy," intoned the professor. "Do not fight it. Relax completely. Allow yourself to go to sleep. To go to sleep and be free."

Now the woman's entire body was shifting from side to side while her eyelids began to flicker erratically. Eventually they closed.

"Now, Margaret, listen to me. You will do as I say. You will obey my commands. Do you understand?"

The woman nodded her head in a neutral fashion as she had done when she had been awake.

The professor turned to us. "There you are, gentlemen, the patient is now hypnotised. It is, I have to admit, a simple procedure with someone like Margaret who has such a feeble grasp of reality, but in essence the procedure is the same with all subjects. Now she is completely under my control. Allow me to demonstrate."

Professor Clark moved towards the small table and, taking a candle from his coat pocket, placed it there and lit it. Returning his attention to his patient, he leaned close to her face. "Margaret, I want you to stand up, walk to the candle on the table and hold your hand over the flame."

With stiff, awkward movements, the woman rose from the bed and made her way slowly towards the table. Without hesitation, she followed Clark's instruction, bringing her hand close to the flickering candle flame as though warming her palm.

"Now, I want you to put your hand down onto the flame. Do not worry, you will feel no pain. I repeat, you will feel no pain."

I was appalled at such an instruction. I could not believe that a respected medical man would treat his patient in such a manner. I made a move forward, but Holmes grabbed my arm and held me back, giving me a stern, imperious shake of the head that informed me not to intervene. With great reluctance, I held my tongue.

Without hesitation, Margaret obeyed Clark's injunction. Her face registered no emotion whatsoever. She held her hand there for some ten seconds before the professor instructed her to remove it. "When you awake," he intoned, "you will feel no pain or have any memory of what you have just done. Now return to the bed."

The woman obeyed.

"Now, Margaret, when I touch your forehead you will awake and remember nothing." He pressed his fingers on the poor creature's head and immediately Margaret shook herself, sloughing off her trance-like state as if it were some invisible garment and then staring blankly before her. She was quite still and showed no sign of pain or distress.

"You see now, Mr. Holmes, the power that hypnotism can evoke and the possibilities it presents for medical operations and experiments."

"Indeed I do."

I remained silent. I was disturbed by what I had seen, which to my mind had been nothing more than a fairground sideshow. The woman had been used as a guinea pig to demonstrate Professor Clark's apparent skill and mastery. In making her act as she did, it seemed to me that Clark had made no allowance for any mental disturbance that might occur as a result of such interference with the patient's free will.

"We are still at the early stages of understanding the power and range of hypnotherapy, but I feel sure that within ten years it will be the leading tool in curing the sick."

"As a criminologist, I can see that the practice may also have uses which are not for the benefit of mankind," observed Holmes. "Control over another human is a very dangerous thing."

"Oh, I agree. Even now hypnotism has a dubious reputation. Already, alas, there are trick hypnotists appearing in the music halls and pseudo-doctors setting up at fashionable addresses in London to cure wealthy ladies of minor problems by a series of auto-suggestions. These charlatans are tainting the professional reputation of the procedure and making it difficult for the discipline and its true practitioners, like myself, to be taken seriously."

"Well, I thank you for your time and kindness in explaining and demonstrating the mechanics of hypnotherapy, Professor," said Holmes, with an appreciative bow. "I wish you great success in your endeavours. And now I think it is time for Watson and I to leave you to your work."

"It has been my pleasure to meet you and a privilege to have been of some assistance to you." He banged on the door of the cell to alert the guard to release us. "I shall escort you to the main foyer. I do hope that your visit has been useful, and I hope that in some future edition of *The Strand* magazine I may read all about your current investigation."

"The fellow is little better than the fairground entertainers he vilified," I said with some warmth as we rode back in a cab to Baker Street. "The way he used that poor creature to demonstrate to us his skills and his power over her was nothing short of disgraceful. The experiment was of no benefit to the woman whatsoever."

"In many ways I agree with you, Watson. But, as a medical man yourself, you know very well that when one is passionate and dedicated to an aspect of one's profession, one may become somewhat immune to the hurt inflicted on human guinea pigs in the course of making progress. And little medical progress is made without such suffering."

For one brief instant I was reminded of a comment that my old friend Stamford had made many years ago, on the day I first met Sherlock Holmes: *Holmes is a little too scientific for my tastes – it approaches to cold-bloodedness.*

"It has been an interesting visit nonetheless," my friend was saying, his voice breaking into my reverie. "I admit the idea of hypnosis remains a tenuous thread in this difficult case, but at least it is a thread."

"Do you really believe that the murderer of Lady Damury and the man who attacked Ruth Marshall were actually hypnotised to carry out these deeds?"

"That is my thinking. Today's visit to St Mary Bethlehem has convinced me that it is possible. The indications are that the attacks were carried out by the same man: his height, his odd gait, the dark hair that I found on both victims."

"Let us suppose that that is the case," said I, "and that the fellow with the walrus moustache and fake hair is the hypnotist. Why should he wish these two women to be murdered? The police have established no apparent link between them. They come from such different spheres of life."

"That is the really puzzling aspect of this case. As you say, there is no obvious connection beyond the fact that both women had lovers, which might indicate some twisted moral judgement. Or, of course, that may be completely coincidental."

"Random killings, then."

Holmes's features darkened at the suggestion. "The worst state of affairs. There is a kind of theatricality about the crimes, indicating that the perpetrator suffers to some extent from mental instability. However, they reveal in addition a certain degree of careful planning, which implies alongside it intelligent cunning and criminality."

"And you believe there are two men involved in the crimes?"

"Yes, I do."

"Then it would seem that the phrase 'looking for a needle in a haystack' was coined especially with reference to this investigation," I mused grimly.

"Quite right, Watson: an apt old saying which is painfully pertinent in this case. And the more I contemplate this devilish business, the more I am unsure whether Miss Ruth Marshall is safe."

"What on earth do you mean?"

"Let me now throw an old saying at you: if at first you don't succeed…"

My blood ran cold at the implication of this statement.

"I think," said Holmes, "it would ease my mind if I took some drastic action in this matter. Therefore I shall need to contact Wiggins of the Irregulars and be especially persuasive with Mrs. Hudson."

Chapter Eighteen

It had never occurred to Caligari at the outset that he should change the rules of his dark game. The pleasure lay in sending his instrument of death into the night to carry out his orders – his orders to kill and then return. The initial test – the death of Lady Damury – had brought him great joy. Things had gone so smoothly the first time, everything according to his finely honed plan. He had remained safe, far away from the murder scene. It was, to his mind, a triumph. Then had come disaster. It had dented his pride. To restore his confidence he must prepare Robert more vigorously, and to ensure success he would alter the conditions of the experiment: not for security purposes alone, but also for extra enjoyment. Why should he absent himself from the final moments and miss the thrilling denouement? Why should he deny himself the satisfaction of witnessing the victim's demise?

Why indeed?

* * *

Once more Gustav Caligari donned the voluminous wig, the walrus moustache and the dark-rimmed spectacles. As he gazed at his reflection in the mirror, he chuckled to himself. Not even his own father would recognise him. That was essential: his anonymity must be protected at all costs. No one must ever suspect his involvement with these murders – the adventure was only just beginning. That he should remain an unknown factor in the crimes was part of the excitement and their *raison d'être*. He had already donned his disguise once again, to discover the girl's current location, and no one had suspected a thing. Of course, he was well aware that to take part in the escapade entailed extra danger. But this also added a frisson of pleasure to the game, pleasure enhanced by the seeds of fear and apprehension that were already germinating in his stomach. His mind thrilled at the idea of seeing the girl die before him. Her eyes would bulge in terror; her mouth would flap open and then close, only the faintest of sounds – a terrified whimpering – emerging as Robert tightened the grip around her neck. Meanwhile, he would stand by, intent, watching the remarkable spectacle with great delight. It would be akin to, but far greater than, the vicarious sensations he had experienced when watching those gothic productions in his youth.

Once more the moon, a new moon on this occasion, prompted the time for action. Now he knew he was ready to raise the curtain on the first act of this delightfully cruel melodrama. It was a performance in which he was to take the leading role. Robert would make his entrance towards the end, to bring about the devastating finale.

Caligari left the house and made his way to the small stable block down the street, where his horse and carriage were housed. He had only just purchased these, realising that he could not rely on cabs for his and Robert's excursions. A private conveyance was ideal: it was an extra form of insurance and granted him more autonomy.

As he walked, the dusk seemed to gather around him like a gloomy amorphous friend, and the bleary gas lamps flicked above him like so many yellow eyes peering into the growing darkness. Night time beckoned. He felt happier, more secure in the shadows, hiding from the light of day.

Some time later Caligari brought the small carriage outside the house and went inside to collect Robert. The young man now existed for the most part in a somnambulistic stupor, requiring little attention except to be fed and exercised, like a dog, to keep up the strength necessary to kill. He had become almost a living doll. Once Robert was safely installed in the carriage, sitting upright and still like an exhibit in Madame Tussaud's waxworks, Caligari set off for Camberwell.

The nursing home was hidden from the road by a thick hedge and a belt of trees. Caligari tied the horse to the gate and inspected his silent passenger, whose bright, vacant eyes shone in the darkness of the cab but exhibited no sign of life or thought.

Taking a deep breath in preparation for his performance, Caligari made his way up the path towards the entrance to the nursing home. He did not see the silhouette of a youth lurking in the shrubbery, watching him with the keenness of a hawk.

The blinds were drawn at every window, but a rich amber glow radiated across the lawn from each one, while a bright lamp illuminated the porch. Before he rang the bell, Caligari made sure that he stood with his back to the light so that his face was cast into shadow.

After a short interval a maid answered the door.

"Good evening," he said, adding a throaty rasp to his own natural tones. "I am Dr. Andrew Dodd, the family physician of the Marshall family. I have come to take Miss Ruth Marshall home."

The maid gave a little curtsey and stood to one side while he entered the hallway. "If you'll just wait here, sir, I will enquire." And then she scuttled off into the innards of the building, returning a couple of minutes later with a large cream envelope.

"I am instructed to inform you that Miss Marshall is no longer a patient here, sir. She has been taken elsewhere. This envelope was left to be given to anyone who made enquiries about the lady."

She passed the envelope to Caligari, who stared at it, dumbfounded. What on earth was this all about? Had his plans been confounded a second time? He ripped open the envelope with some urgency and withdrew a single sheet of writing paper. It bore the message in a firm clear script:

> *Miss Marshall is in safe hands.*
> *Sherlock Holmes*

Caligari stared at the missive in shock and amazement. Then he crumpled the paper up in anger and, without a word, turned and left the building. He hurried down the path muttering quiet oaths to himself.

The figure in the shrubbery slipped out from the shadows and followed Caligari at a distance. Crouching by the gate, he waited until Caligari had clambered aboard the carriage before slipping into the road, and pulled himself up into a crouching position at the rear of the vehicle. His grip was tenuous. His thin fingers clung to two hooks on the back of the carriage that were used to secure the leather straps holding luggage in place on the roof, while his legs were pulled up only inches above the road. With a sudden jerk, the carriage pulled away, almost dislodging its secret passenger. *This*, thought Wiggins, *is going to be a terrible journey.*

Chapter Nineteen

From the journal of Dr. John H. Watson

There was a tap at our sitting-room door and Holmes bade our visitor enter. It was Alan Firbank. With his necktie askew and his crumpled suit, he presented a rather dishevelled figure, whose features revealed all too cruelly the strain he was undergoing.

"I've just left Ruth. She seems to be rallying well, thanks to Mrs. Hudson's care and attention. She assures me she'll keep a constant watchful eye on Ruth. I think I shall sleep a little more soundly tonight knowing that she is under your protection, Mr. Holmes," he said with great emotion.

"Bringing her to Baker Street was a sensible precaution," observed my friend. "The man who attempted to snuff out her young life may very well try again. She is certainly safer here than in the nursing home, where she made a very vulnerable target."

Firbank shook his head sadly. "But I still cannot fathom why anyone should wish to harm Ruth. What can be the motive?"

"I am afraid to say that I do not know – for the moment at least. But fear not, I am sure I shall unearth the truth in due course."

"I do hope so. Well, gentlemen, I shall be away to my own bed, but with your indulgence I shall call on Ruth in the morning to check on her progress."

"Of course," said Holmes. "Feel free to come and see her whenever you like. Now go and get a good night's rest."

After the young man had departed, Holmes re-lit his pipe and frowned at me. "Our friend Firbank was right, of course."

"In what sense?" I said.

"To ask me what is the motive. That is often the guiding light that leads one to a solution. But in this instance we have nothing. One cannot apply logic where there appears to be none."

I was about to respond when there came another tap at the door.

"Surely, this cannot be Firbank returning," I said.

Holmes shrugged and called to the visitor to enter. In walked a bedraggled youth with a grimy visage and muddied clothing.

"By all that's wonderful, Wiggins!" cried Holmes. "You look as though you have been brawling in the street."

"I wish I had. I'd 'ave come off better than I did with the kerbstone." As he finished the sentence, his knees buckled and he sank to the floor. "Bleedin' 'ell!" he cried.

"Quick, Watson, the brandy," said Holmes, rushing to the youth's aid and helping him into a chair.

"Sorry, Mr. 'Olmes," he muttered. "I don't know what came over me."

"That's all right, Wiggins. You have clearly been in the wars."

Wiggins gave a half-hearted smile. "Not the wars, sir, just fallin' off the back of a carriage."

I pressed a brandy glass into his hand. "Take a few sips of that. It will help restore your equilibrium," I said gently.

The boy's smile widened. "I didn't know I had any of that,

Doctor," he said, before taking a large gulp of brandy. "Phew!" he said, spluttering. "That's fire in a glass, that is."

Holmes smiled and returned to his seat. "Now then, Wiggins," he said, "do you feel up to telling us all about it? You obviously have a rare tale to tell."

Wiggins nodded and drained the glass. "I certainly have. It's like this: I did as you asked me and set meself up as sentry at the nursing home down Camberwell way. Settled down in the bushes at the far end of the garden with a good view of the front door. There were a few comings and goings but nothing what you might call suspicious-like. Certainly there was no gent callin' with all that hair and the large moustache as you'd mentioned, Mr. H. That is, not until around nine o'clock." At this juncture, Wiggins produced a shiny pocket watch from his shabby waistcoat to give evidence of how he could be so accurate as to the time.

Holmes nodded appreciatively and Wiggins returned the watch to its safe lodging. "So, there he was. A big bloke with that hair and 'tache. I crept a little closer as he rang the bell so's I could hear what he was goin' ter say. The maid came to the door and he said he was a Dr. Dodd and had come to take that girl, Miss Ruth Marshall, back to the bosom of her family."

"Did he, now," said Holmes, an expression of dark amusement touching his gaunt features.

"He weren't best pleased when he heard she'd gone. The maid gave him a letter. I don't know what it said but it certainly made him mad and he screwed the paper up. Soon after he stormed off down the path to his carriage. Oh, yes, I forgot to mention he came in his own carriage. He was the driver."

"Was he? Did you happen to see whether there was a passenger inside?"

"I did later on, yes. All I could tell you was that it was a man. It was dark and he was back in the shadows of the cab. He didn't say nothing, or move at all as far as I could tell. Anyway, I knew I had to act fast. The hairy fellow was up in the driver's seat in a trice, so I ran round to the back of the cab to get meself a free ride. I was sure as you'd want to learn where the cove lived."

"Indeed," said Holmes enthusiastically.

"Well, there was very little to grab hold of, but I managed after a fashion. I tell you, Mr. 'Olmes, it was a treacherous journey. My hands are red raw. And the blighter drove at such a speed. He went round corners as if he were in a race. I was nearly thrown off more than once. Then, of course, it did happen. We had just got into Knightsbridge when the carriage turned suddenly with such a ruddy sharp motion spinnin' round a corner. Well, I lost my grip and my balance and I fell off, banging my head on the pavement and then rolling into a muddy puddle."

"Oh, my poor fellow," I cried.

"Indeed, commiserations, Wiggins. You have acted beyond the call of duty. I am most appreciative of your efforts."

"But I let you down, sir. I didn't get to know his address."

"Do not fret about that. I am sure it will come to light in due course."

"As I say, I didn't manage to stay with him till he got to his lair, but I did get to put a mark on the back of the carriage so I'd recognise it again."

"Did you, by Jove!" cried Holmes, rubbing his hands enthusiastically.

Wiggins beamed with a mischievous twinkle in his eye. "Yeah, I managed to put a big chalk mark on the back in the shape of a cross. If you see a carriage with one of those on, you'll know you've got your man."

"That is quite excellent, Wiggins. Deserving of another sovereign." Sherlock Holmes reached inside his trouser pocket, extracted a gold coin and tossed it to the Baker Street Irregular.

"Ta. Very much obliged, Mr. 'Olmes."

"No, Wiggins, it is I who am very much obliged. You have managed to provide me with essential information this evening. I am in your debt. Now, you say that when you were dislodged from the carriage you were in Knightsbridge?"

"Yes, just off the Brompton Road."

Holmes made a note of this, scribbling details on his cuff.

"How are you feeling now?" I asked the bedraggled youth.

"Oh, I'm all right, Doctor. Nearly back to me normal self. But I wouldn't mind another glass of your medicine to send me on my way."

I grinned and obliged the fellow, inspecting him meanwhile to ensure that he had come to no serious harm. He downed the brandy in one gulp and got to his feet. "Well, gentlemen, if I can be of no further assistance…"

Holmes rose also. "You have done sterling work, for which I thank you. Go home now and get a good night's rest. I will be in touch if I need you again."

Wiggins grinned and gave a salute. "Right you are, guv. Happy to be of help," he said, jingling his pockets, and then was on his way.

"Well, Holmes," I said when we were alone once more, "it seems that your theory is bearing fruit. What a pity Wiggins was unable to hang on to the carriage until it reached its destination."

"Yes, that is unfortunate. But the problem is not insurmountable. And we have the marked carriage to console us. It will give me some investigative work to carry out tomorrow. We know it is probable that our murderer resides somewhere in the Knightsbridge area. It should not be beyond the bounds of my ingenuity to discover the exact whereabouts."

I raised my eyebrows in surprise at this statement. "Well, the haystack in which the needle is hidden is now considerably smaller, but it is still a haystack," I observed.

Holmes chuckled. "Oh, ye of little faith, Watson. We shall see what the morrow brings. Black carriages with a large white cross on their rear are, I believe, a rarity in London. In the meantime may I suggest you go down to Mrs. Hudson's quarters and check on your patient one last time before you retire."

I did as requested and found Miss Marshall fast asleep. Her pulse and temperature were normal and her complexion had lost the waxen pallor it had when I first saw her. "She had some soup and a chicken salad for supper," Mrs. Hudson informed me. "I think she's really on the mend. We had a little chat earlier and she seemed quite normal. How long do you think she'll be staying with us?"

I shrugged my shoulders. "I cannot be sure. While the man who tried to kill her is still at large it would not be safe for her to return to her own quarters, or resume her role in the theatre. We have to catch the blighter first."

"With Mr. Holmes on the case, that can't be long, I imagine."

I did not share Mrs. Hudson's sanguinity concerning this complicated investigation, and so I merely gave her a weak smile in response.

It was time for me to leave. I thanked her heartily for her ministrations and then made my way up to my bedroom. In passing our sitting-room door, I could hear the melancholy strains of Holmes's violin. He was obviously intent on keeping a midnight vigil.

Chapter Twenty

Gustav Caligari, too, was far from ready to retire to his bedroom. The anger that had taken hold of him when he learned that his plans had been thwarted – thwarted by none other than Sherlock Holmes – had festered within him like a canker. This fury, coupled with the frustration that he felt regarding the failure of that evening's mission, wracked his body. It brought him physical pain, to such an extent that he was barely able to sit still. He paced the floor of his small consulting room, hands thrust deep into his pockets, muttering a mixture of dark thoughts and foul oaths.

"Sherlock Holmes!" he barked occasionally in his perambulations, as though the name were a curse. It was all Holmes's fault that his plans had been thrown into disarray. Of course he knew the man by reputation. Which Londoner didn't? Sherlock Holmes, the so-called brilliant private detective. He had a string of successful cases to his name. Criminals went in fear of him and the police were in awe of him. *Well, I neither fear nor revere the scoundrel,* thought Caligari, bringing his fist down hard on his desk.

Caligari had never contemplated for one moment that their paths would cross. He harboured no insecurities regarding Holmes, he was simply enraged that the fellow's actions had disrupted his plans so effectively. His careful preparations to snatch Ruth Marshall and watch her die had come to naught – all because of Sherlock Holmes. The thought bore into his brain and he cried aloud in fury. Seizing a decanter of whisky from the sideboard, he snatched off the stopper and downed a long draught of the liquid straight from the neck, deliberately allowing it to burn his throat and make him splutter. Strangely, the discomfort caused him to smile.

At length he sat down, and in more civilised fashion poured more whisky into a glass before consuming it. Gradually, as the effects took hold, his temper calmed and he began to think in more rational terms. How was he to resolve his dilemma? What was he to do now? He strove hard to corral the various diverse thoughts that crowded his mind. He knew that he must be practical and logical in his actions – emotional decisions would only lead to disaster – but he was also very sure that he had in some way to ameliorate his disappointment. Once more, he turned his attention towards Sherlock Holmes. *Whatever I do*, Caligari thought, *Holmes must in some way suffer and experience the sourness of failure and defeat. That damned fellow shall not beat me; I shall defeat him.* At this thought he gave a small cry of satisfaction. Indeed, to cause deep discomfort to the Great Detective would bring him great joy and to some extent help to eliminate the pain he now felt.

Another glass of whisky passed his lips while he contemplated this premise. As usual, all must be secret. All must be conducted without giving the slightest hint as to the identity of the perpetrator, the supreme puppet master. He nodded sagely in his intoxication.

But what was he to do? It was obvious that it would be foolish, and most likely fatal, to attempt to discover the whereabouts of Ruth Marshall and make a second attempt on her life. That would be too dangerous and might easily lead to exposure. Holmes would have her hidden somewhere. He was like a spider on his web, waiting for the unwary fly. He would have it all set up: an intricate and sophisticated trap.

Well, the devil Holmes would be disappointed. Gustav Caligari was not about to take on the role of fly, seeking to end Miss Ruth Marshall's life once more. Mr. Detective Holmes could wait in the shadows until he rotted.

The cogs of Caligari's mind, amply lubricated by the oil of alcohol, began turning swiftly and a fantastical notion came to him. Yes, of course, he would strike elsewhere, while old Holmes was playing guardian angel to Miss Ruth Marshall. He would effect a different kind of blow on his enemy. If he could not eliminate the wretched girl, he would pick the next best thing.

Caligari's eyes brightened as he contemplated the possibility and his lips parted in a ghoulish leer. Of course, that was it. That was what he would do. This particular plan, which seemed to fall into place in seconds, would not only bring him enormous satisfaction but would bring great discomfort to that infernal meddler, Sherlock Holmes.

Caligari knew he must act quickly. Immediately, in fact. For his own sense of satisfaction, at least. The sooner he caused an upset in the life of that damned interfering detective the better. And it would be a very serious upset. It was not yet eleven in the evening and his plan was already formulated. He intended to carry it out that very night. By dawn, the deed would be done. His brain was sparking now. Energy, alcohol and hatred mixed in a potent brew to fuel his twisted imagination. The mechanics, he knew, were easy. Speed was of the essence. Within half an hour, Caligari had roused Robert and placed him in the carriage, and was traversing the midnight streets of London on his way to Paddington.

It was nearly one o'clock by the time he reached his destination: a smart road of small, respectable suburban terraced houses. They stood silent and dark in the delicate moonlight which beamed down from a cloudless sky. He pulled into a side street and tethered the horse. Inside the carriage, he gave his instructions to Robert once more, slowly and deliberately. There must be no mistakes this time. His puppet was to carry out his instructions whatever obstacles he might encounter. The somnambulist's unblinking eyes stared into the darkness as Caligari's forceful words registered themselves in his mind: "Go now. Go now and kill."

Slowly, with stiff awkward movements, Robert left the carriage and made his way towards his destination.

Blanche Andrews was roused from a particularly pleasant dream in which she was visiting her mother's house in Ireland and giving her a warm embrace. Despite the fact that her mother had been dead for seven years, the dream seemed so real. She felt the smooth skin of her mother's face against her cheek and caught the faint smell of rosemary that always seemed to accompany her. And then some raucous commotion from downstairs propelled her into wakefulness. There was another sound, and she sat up in bed, at first puzzled rather than concerned. She strained her ears for further disturbance. There seemed to be none at the outset, but moments later, she heard a sound that sent a chill of fear through her whole being. Footsteps, moving up the stairs with a slow, heavy tread. Instinctively, she jumped out of bed, reached for her robe –

and then stood frozen with fear. She had no idea what to do next. The footsteps grew nearer, and the handle of her bedroom door turned. She gave a small whimper of distress as she saw the door open, slowly revealing the intruder.

Standing before her was a tall, dark figure of a man who, on sensing her presence in the gloom, moved towards her with a strange, stiffened gait. The fact that she was unable to see his face made him all the more terrifying. She screamed, the sound quickly stifled by the strong fingers that clutched her throat and pressed hard on her windpipe. She tried to struggle. She tried to pull free of his grasp. She tried to fight back, but his grip was unyielding and soon she began to lose consciousness. A roaring sound, rather like waves crashing on the seashore, filled her ears, while a shifting, dark grey mist began to fog her vision. For a brief moment an image of her mother rose up before her eyes and then disappeared. It was at this moment that she knew she was about to die, and there was nothing she could do to prevent it.

Within seconds, Blanche had become like a rag doll in the hands of her assailant. Her head lolled backwards, her mouth agape, her thick moist tongue protruding. Robert hauled her limp frame over to the bed and laid it down, gently, on the rumpled bedcovers. For some moments he stared down at her. His features remained immobile but the eyes flickered brightly, indicating the vague pleasure that he felt – pleasure at carrying out his master's instructions successfully. Then, from the inside pocket of his jacket, he extracted the sheet of paper that Caligari had given him and laid it down with great reverence on the chest of the corpse. Now his mission was complete, he turned quickly and left the room.

Blanche Andrews lay dead on the bed, her sightless eyes gazing at the ceiling.

Chapter Twenty-one

From the journal of Dr. John H. Watson

I rose early and visited my patient, Ruth Marshall. She was well on the way to recovery. The colour had returned to her cheeks and she had lost that strained nervous manner she had exhibited when first I saw her. It seemed to me that she had blanked from her mind her unpleasant experience and was looking forward to returning to normal life and to the theatre. I was uncertain whether Holmes would allow her to do so before her would-be murderer was apprehended. As I left her room, Alan Firbank arrived to see her, carrying a large bunch of flowers. He also seemed in a far more cheerful frame of mind now that he knew Miss Marshall was safe and making a sound recovery. We exchanged a few pleasantries before I returned to our sitting room.

I found Holmes still in a meditative mood. Indeed, he eschewed any food or conversation and simply smoked his old briar and drank black coffee. I knew that on such occasions it was best to leave him to his own contemplations. He certainly would not welcome any attempts on my part to involve him in discussing the case. I had no wish to derail any of his trains of thought. Instead, I satisfied myself with a boiled egg and some of Mrs. Hudson's excellent buttered muffins.

I had an instant before pushed my plate away and was contemplating joining Holmes in the first pipe of the day, when there came a heavy knock at our door and without waiting for a reply, our visitor entered. It was Inspector Lestrade. He seemed a ragged ghost of his usual self. In general, he was smartly dressed and tidy in appearance. This morning he presented a much-altered image. His tie was askew, his suit rumpled and his features haggard, with dark circles beneath his eyes. The growth of stubble on his chin, meanwhile, suggested that it had not seen a razor for at least twenty-four hours.

"Sorry to burst in on you like this, Mr. Holmes," he said in breathless tones, "but there's something you ought to know."

"I gathered as much from your rather dramatic entrance," observed my friend, languidly. "Do take a seat, Lestrade, while you get your breath back. Watson, be a good chap and pour the inspector a cup of café noir. I can see that he needs something to help him keep awake. He has been up since the early hours of the morning involved in some terrible crime."

"How d'you know that?" Lestrade asked, slumping down in the wicker chair near the fire. "Go on, amaze me."

Holmes smiled. "Your unkempt appearance indicates that you dressed in a hurry. By the state of your collar, I should say that was yesterday's adornment, reached for as you were roused from your slumbers. Your tired features suggest worry and lack of sleep. Why would a police inspector be dragged from his bed in the small hours other than to investigate a serious crime? Obviously the incident is terrible and mystifying, otherwise you would not be calling on me in such a distressed state."

"I am not in a distressed state," the policeman protested. "I am just a little... nonplussed."

Holmes and I exchanged knowing glances.

I passed Lestrade a cup of coffee, which he received gratefully.

"Tell us all about it," said Holmes, sitting back in his chair and steepling his fingers.

"There's been a murder in Paddington. A young woman strangled – very much in the same way that Lady Damury was dispatched. She had those sharp indentations around her throat that you pointed out to me before – marks from long fingernails."

Holmes's eyes flickered with keen interest.

Lestrade continued. "A constable on night duty was passing the house and saw that the front door was wide open. On inspection, he discovered that the lock was broken and a forced entry had been effected. He made his way into the building to investigate further and on the upper floor he made the terrible discovery. In one of the bedrooms he discovered the body of a young woman. She was laid on the bed and the savage marks around the throat indicated that she had been strangled. But that was not all. There was a sheet of paper lying on the woman's chest with a message from the murderer."

"A message. Indeed. What did it say?"

In response, Lestrade pulled a sheet of paper from his overcoat pocket and passed it to Holmes. "You can read it for yourself," he said.

Holmes did so and gave a gasp of surprise. He handed the note to me. I read the scrawled handwriting with shocked amazement:

Sherlock Holmes is to blame for this.

"What can it mean?" I asked.

"Search me," muttered the inspector, shaking his head.

"Tell me," said Holmes, "what was the address where the girl was murdered, and this note found?"

Lestrade consulted his notebook. "Forty-seven Robin Terrace, Paddington."

Holmes clapped his hands with what I can only describe as pleasure. "That is the address where Ruth Marshall lodges. The young woman's name?"

"Blanche Andrews."

Holmes nodded.

"Blimey," cried Lestrade. "Did he think he was having another go at the poor girl?"

Holmes shook his head. "No, no, not all. It very much looks as if our killer, in frustration at failing to end Miss Marshall's life, decided to settle for the next best thing: to murder her fellow lodger."

"You're not serious," cried Lestrade.

"Oh, but I am. We are dealing not only with a cunning and clever murderer, but one whom I am convinced is also mentally unhinged. This message alone indicates as much. It is a tit-for-tat reply in return for the note which I left at the nursing home."

Lestrade scratched his head. "What note at the nursing home? I'm confused."

"It scarcely matters at this moment, but the claim that 'Sherlock Holmes is to blame for this' clearly indicates that the murderer sees my involvement in the case as a great obstacle to his plans. The fact that I removed Miss Marshall from his clutches and prevented his second attempt on her life frustrated him greatly, and he saw killing someone close to her as his revenge on me."

"That is grotesque," I observed. "If what you say is true, the fellow is a madman."

"Probably so," agreed Holmes. "That does not help our case, for it is not easy to anticipate the machinations of such a mind. I fear that my involvement with the case may well have made matters worse."

"How do you make that out, Mr. Holmes?"

"I seem to have given him another purpose, a focus for these killings. I fear there will be further deaths, accompanied by other notes taunting me."

"Well, if you are right, something must be done about this at once."

Holmes gave a wry smile. "But what? Who can say where he will strike again? It would seem that all he requires is a vulnerable female to satisfy his blood lust, and there are thousands in this city of ours. He may strike again anywhere, or at any time."

At this pronouncement we all fell silent for some time. At length, Lestrade rose from his chair with a loud sigh. "Well, I'd better get on with my duties – and keep my fingers crossed that you come up with some idea of how we can track this blighter down."

"I will do my best," said Holmes.

After Lestrade had departed, I sat opposite my friend and asked quietly, "Is it really as hopeless as you indicated to Lestrade?"

Holmes stared at me for some moments before replying. "*Nil desperandum*, my dear Watson. *Nil desperandum.*"

Chapter Twenty-Two

❧

Gustav Caligari stared down at the comatose figure of Robert, who lay like a corpse, hands crossed over his chest, his bloodless face ash-white in repose.

"You have done well. Superbly well, Robert. You have made your master very happy," Caligari intoned with repressed glee and laughed. It was the eerie gurgle of an unstable mind. Slowly he leaned over and took hold of Robert's two hands in his. He caressed them as a lover would his paramour. "You have brought such joy into my life, Robert. You have fulfilled my dreams. We have achieved a wonderfully dark greatness and we shall go on and achieve more. I am the genius and you are the instrument of my success." He bent forward and kissed each finger before replacing Robert's hands upon his chest.

"I shall let you rest for a few days while I ponder my next move. I need to concoct an even more challenging death to frustrate and humiliate Mr. Sherlock Holmes." He laughed again, in the strange high-pitched fashion that he had developed in the last few days. Reality was gradually being obscured by the shadows of his madness.

He moved downstairs to his tiny sitting room, poured himself a large glass of wine and began to think. "Sherlock Holmes," he murmured to himself several times. He must learn more about this supposedly brilliant detective. Only that way could he be fully aware of the man's weaknesses and vulnerable points. Such knowledge was essential if his next murderous project were to succeed. The glass drained, he replenished it to the brim and raised it in a toast. "To Mr. Sherlock Holmes," he intoned. "May God have mercy on your soul – for I certainly shall not." And then he gave another grotesque laugh.

Caligari's investigations into Holmes's career were fruitful. He read copiously about the detective and learned quickly how he operated. The hypnotist came to believe that he could reclaim the upper hand by setting a trap to ensnare the interfering sleuth. A new plan was swiftly engendered and the following afternoon, Caligari stood in a small empty office in Cedar Court, off Marylebone High Street. It was a dusty, cramped little room devoid of fixtures and fittings but Carruthers – the young, arrogant land agent – knew all too well that the office was situated in a prime area of the city. He had no need to make apologies for the cobwebs and peeling wallpaper. Its location at the hub of the West End would sell it to this prospective client without any effort on his part.

Caligari explained that he would need the premises for only one month, and when he had been quoted the exorbitant rent he nodded, accepting the terms without demur. It was an investment which would bring him a great deal of pleasure.

"May I ask for what purpose you intend to use these premises?" asked Carruthers, extracting a contract from his briefcase.

"You may ask," said Caligari.

Carruthers looked blankly at him, faintly unnerved.

Caligari smiled at the young man's discomfort. "I shall be running a medical practice."

"Just for a month?"

"Indeed. Just for a month." He produced an envelope from his overcoat pocket and handed it to Carruthers. "Here is the agreed fee in cash. There is no need to count it. I can assure you it is correct. Now if you will pass me the contract, I shall conclude this transaction and be about my business."

"Why, yes," said Carruthers, stuffing the envelope in his briefcase and passing the document to his new client.

Caligari signed the contract and handed it back to Carruthers.

"Thank you, Mr. Rubenstein," the young man said, scrutinising the name. "Here are the keys. The place is now yours for the next month."

Chapter Twenty-three

From the journal of Dr. John H. Watson

After consuming a selection of the assorted dottles from the mantelpiece in the black clay pipe which was his favourite counsellor, Sherlock Holmes retired to his room without a word. I knew that at this stage of the investigation, I could be of no real assistance to my friend. It was at the time of action that I could best provide support, and so I planned to visit my club for the day. I thought that a change of atmosphere and possibly a game of billiards might help refresh my brain and allow me to gain a new perspective on this most challenging case.

I was about to retrieve my bowler, coat and stick from the hat stand in preparation for my departure when Sherlock Holmes returned to the sitting room. I say that Holmes returned, but that is not quite accurate. A shifty-looking soul, stooped in posture and dressed in a dark, shabby overcoat, shuffled into the chamber. He wore a battered billycock with grey whiskers spreading down either side of his face almost to his chin. His cheeks were rubicund, as was his nose. The figure looked for all the world like a fellow who was down on his luck and sought solace in drink.

"Morning, guv'nor," he croaked, raising his mittened hand to his hat in a mock salute. I had seen many of Holmes's disguises over the years, but this was surely among his most convincing. Had I encountered this sad creature in the street, I may well have passed him a small coin out of sympathy, but I would never have recognised the decrepit wretch as my old friend. I could not help but laugh out loud and applaud the miraculous transformation.

Holmes stood erect and smiled. "You approve, then?" he said cheerfully in his own voice.

"Better than Irving! Your own mother would not recognise you."

"Such a creature as I have become, one of many similar unfortunates in this city of ours, may pass along its streets virtually unnoticed. I am one of the miserable scraps of humanity who have no perch in society and so are ignored by its more fortunate members. My disguise will allow me to move freely and invisibly while I carry out my investigations."

"And what are they?"

"I am to visit Knightsbridge and search its streets and byways in search of a carriage with two hooks and a white cross on the back. Yes, yes, I know, old friend. Your metaphor concerning that needle in the proverbial haystack is already trembling on your lips; and, indeed, you may well be right. But one has to try. I am well aware that it only takes a zealous coachman to have cleaned the vehicle and we are lost. However, when crumbs are few, as they are in this case, one has to rely on persistence and luck."

I nodded in firm agreement. Holmes was right. When times were desperate, desperate measures must be employed. "Is there anything I can do to help?"

Holmes shook his head. "Not at the moment. You go and enjoy your day at the club."

"How did you know that was my intention?"

"You have slipped our copy of *The Times* into the side pocket of your jacket. It is a habit of yours when you go to the club – an insurance that you will have something to read in case their copy is already in the hands of another member."

"Of course. Well, happy hunting. I will see you this evening."

"That you will, sir," Holmes replied in his adopted hoarse whisper, assuming his bent posture. And with another feeble salute, he shuffled out of the room.

My day at the club was dull. Certainly the visit did not achieve its aim. My mind kept returning to the strange and puzzling case in which we were involved. To me, the mystery seemed impenetrable, and it preyed on my mind. I ate a light lunch and then I was joined in the bar by my old friend, Thurston. Later we engaged in a game of billiards, but my concentration was so poor that he had no trouble in thrashing me soundly.

Wearily, I returned to Baker Street around five in the evening. I called in on Mrs. Hudson and found her sitting by her cheery fire, chatting to Ruth Marshall. The young lady now appeared to be much recovered. She had dispensed with the attire of the sick bed and was dressed in a dark green velvet costume. She looked charming.

On seeing me, she beamed brightly and immediately began to question me as to when she might return to her lodgings. She was very eager to resume her normal life, but I could see from the dark shadows beneath her eyes and the pallor of her complexion that she was still far from being restored to full health and vigour. I knew that I must not alert the girl to the news that her fellow lodger had been killed. The revelation could easily send her spinning back into a distressed state. It was equally clear to me, however, that even discounting this terrible incident, it was not safe for the girl to leave Baker Street as long as the killer was at large. I made the point in the gentlest and least dramatic terms, emphasising that it was with her safety and best interests at heart that both Holmes and I believed that she should stay under our roof a little longer.

Somewhat reluctantly she accepted my argument, but I could see that it made her unhappy. She was a young woman on the brink of an exciting acting career and she wanted to be getting on with it. She had no real knowledge of the nature of the twisted individual who had made one attempt on her life, or the threat that he still posed. Holmes was certain, I knew, that, given an opportunity, the devil would try again. While in Baker Street, under our watchful supervision, she was secure; that was the main thing. Assuring her of our best attention, it was with some relief that I made my way up the seventeen steps to our sitting room.

Holmes had not yet returned, so I sat patiently by the fireside smoking a pipe and awaiting his arrival. Around seven, I heard his familiar tread on the stair and moments later, the old derelict entered the room with a heavy sigh. Despite his make-up I could see that my friend was weary and his expression gave me little hope that he had achieved any success in his venture.

"Pour me a brandy, old chap," he said in his normal voice. "I'll just dispose of this character and be with you in five minutes." It was nearer a quarter of an hour before he returned to our sitting room, wrapped in his mouse-coloured dressing gown. All signs of his assumed persona had disappeared and the fine gaunt features were unadorned by greasepaint and whiskers. Taking up the glass of brandy I had poured for him, he flung himself down in his usual chair opposite me. "As you may gather from my demeanour, Watson, my efforts have been fruitless. I have travelled every street, road, avenue and cul-de-sac within a mile of where Wiggins was dislodged from the carriage. I was looking for premises that might house such a carriage or, if I was fortunate, the carriage itself. I was not fortunate enough."

"Well, it may be that the villain was only passing through Knightsbridge, and his destination was further afield."

"Of course, of course. And if that is the case your haystack has grown to tremendous proportions." He took a sip of brandy and sighed.

"Where does this leave us?" I asked.

"In a very precarious situation. There are no clues to help us. We are in the dark. I think tomorrow I will seek Lestrade's permission to visit Paddington, the scene of the recent murder. It is possible I might find something there that will help to light our way to future action."

"We can but hope," said I.

"Sadly, hope is the best we have at present," responded my friend wearily.

In all the cases that I had been involved in with Sherlock Holmes, I was unable to remember a time when he appeared so despondent and frustrated regarding his lack of progress. Both of us, I believed, harboured the dark thought that this investigation might not move forward at all until there was another victim.

The case took a dramatic and unexpected turn the following morning. We had breakfasted early and were preparing to see

Lestrade when there came a loud, insistent ring on our doorbell. I gazed out of the window and observed standing on our doorstep a tall, stout man wearing a fedora and large black overcoat with an astrakhan collar. I had not seen him before and I assumed that he must be a potential client. When I conveyed the information to Holmes, he groaned.

"That is the last thing I want now. My mind and time are completely devoted to this baffling murder case; I cannot take on other considerations."

"Well, at least you can see the man," I said. "A fresh challenge may in some way help your thought processes…"

Holmes gave a sarcastic bellow. "Sometimes, Watson, you talk the most utter rot."

Before I was able to respond there came a gentle knock on the door. Holmes raised his brow in resigned frustration. "Enter," he cried.

Our visitor was the man I had observed on the step moments earlier. He was well-built, with a pugnacious expression and startling blue eyes. His complexion was coarse and his face had a fine layer of perspiration on it, which I suspected was a permanent feature. He whipped off his hat to reveal a large head with cropped hair, which was beginning to grey at the temples.

"Mr. Holmes? Mr. Sherlock Holmes?" He gazed at each of us in turn before settling his attention on my friend. "I do hope you can give me some advice and help. I am in desperate need of both."

Without a word, Holmes gestured to the man to take a seat.

"Thank you," he said. Although he spoke in clear, moderated tones, there was the trace of a foreign accent in his voice. "I am Alexander Rubenstein. Doctor Alexander Rubenstein. I have a private practice in London and I have come to consult you about one of my patients."

"Then consult," said Holmes sharply, not masking his irritation at having to cope with a new client at this time.

"I refer to a fellow Austrian – a new patient of mine. His name is Robert Strauss. I am very concerned about him. He came to me because he was suffering from extreme sleep deprivation. Chronic insomnia. I gave him some sedative powders but apparently they were not effective in relieving his malady." Our visitor gave a bleak smile. "The fellow began to haunt my consulting room. I think he saw it as a kind of confessional chamber."

"Confessional?" said Holmes.

"Yes. He began to tell me things about himself that unnerved me. He has a dark and perverted imagination. It has become clear that it is his own guilty nature which has prevented him from sleeping at night. His cruel, unnatural thoughts prevent the onset of sleep, which as Shakespeare has it 'is the balm of hurt minds'."

"What sort of things did he tell you that made you uncomfortable? Pray be clear and precise."

"That is the problem, Mr. Holmes. I am unable to be precise. He told me nothing in concrete terms."

"Yet you use the words 'confessional' and 'guilty', and refer to his thoughts as cruel and unnatural. Why?"

Rubenstein gave a heavy shrug of the shoulders. "It is so difficult for me to explain. In my consulting room, the fellow relaxes and then rambles in an unnerving, delirious fashion. From his tired brain tumble many strange snatches of conversation, weird imagery. He made references to strangling, to squeezing the fine flesh of a young woman's throat. When I asked if he had ever done such a thing, he denied it vehemently, but he looked at me in such an odd way as he spoke that I was of the strong opinion that he was not being completely honest. He also told me that when unable to sleep he would often walk the deserted streets and stare in at the windows of darkened houses, envious of the sleepers inside. 'They make me mad with their easy slumbers,' he said. 'It makes me want to kill them.'"

"I see," said Holmes. "Obviously the man is greatly disturbed and needs treatment. But why have you come to me? Surely he needs a doctor, not a detective. What do you think I can do?"

"I have a horrible feeling that this man has killed, and that he may well kill again. I believe that these fantastic scenes that he conjures up have actually taken place. They are crimes of violence and murder, and yet I have no definite proof. As a result I cannot go to the police authorities. I am sure they would laugh at me or at best think I was delusional."

"And what makes you think that I will react any differently?"

"Because you are much shrewder. I have read of your work and I know that you can see beyond the obvious, see things that others are unable to see. That you are able to uncover secret truths which lie hidden from the eyes of the official investigators."

Holmes gave a bleak smile. "You make me sound quite a paragon. You have obviously been overdosing on Dr. Watson's accounts of my doings. He tends to exaggerate my skills somewhat. However, I am still not clear why you think this patient of yours may be a murderer."

Rubenstein screwed up his face. "It is so difficult to explain. I suppose it is more intuition than... Yesterday, for example, he came to me in quite a dishevelled state after another night without sleep. He sat in the chair opposite my desk, his long fingers working frantically all the time he was talking to me, as though, as though... as though he were strangling someone." Our visitor demonstrated the actions in a melodramatic fashion before continuing, pressing his podgy fingers around an imaginary throat. "He told me that his insomnia had led him to walk the streets again. Apparently he found himself in Paddington at one point, before losing track of reality. The next thing he remembered was finding himself sitting on his own doorstep as dawn was breaking. He had no notion of what had happened in the meantime. Then I read in the papers that a young woman had been murdered – strangled – in the Paddington area. I could not help but put the two incidents together. Surely it cannot simply be a coincidence?" He shook his head vigorously. "I really do not know what to do, Mr. Holmes."

My friend glanced at me. It was a gesture of enquiry, soliciting my view of the garbled but chilling recitative we had just heard. I gave a little shake of the head, hoping to convey the sense that I was perplexed by the tale and was entirely unsure what Holmes should do about it.

"Where does your patient live?" asked my friend at length.

"That is part of the problem. I do not know. He never revealed this information to me. It is not a requirement I make for receiving treatment. I am new to the city and I am keen to take on as many patients as possible to establish my practice. They come to me for consultation; I do not make house calls."

"So you have no way of tracing him?"

Rubenstein shook his head.

"Then I do not know what you expect me to do. I am afraid the details of your concern are nebulous. I suggest you come back to me when you have something more concrete to relay. I am a very busy man and am currently engaged on a most important case and I cannot spare any time to go chasing will-o'-the-wisps."

"But Mr. Holmes... I fear... Look, Mr. Strauss has an appointment to see me tomorrow at four-thirty in the afternoon. Is it possible for you also to be in attendance and judge for yourself whether my suspicions are well founded or, as you state, a mere will-o'-the-wisp?"

Holmes thought for a moment. "Very well. I will attend this consultation."

"Oh, thank you, thank you. That is marvellous. It will set my mind at ease, but..." Our visitor hesitated and seemed somewhat reluctant to continue.

"But...?" prompted Holmes.

"Well, I think it would be best if you came alone. I fear that two extra persons in my consulting room might well put Mr. Strauss on his guard. I could introduce you as an esteemed colleague."

"I am sure Dr. Watson would be more than happy to sit out this particular investigation."

"Of course. Whatever is for the best," I averred.

"That is arranged, then. If you will be at my consulting rooms some twenty minutes before Mr. Strauss's appointment at four-thirty p.m...." Rubenstein handed Holmes his card.

"I shall be there," confirmed Holmes, slipping the card into his waistcoat pocket.

"Excellent. Well, gentlemen, I will not take up any more of your valuable time." He rose swiftly and made for the door. "Your co-operation has eased my mind greatly, Mr. Holmes. I cannot thank you enough. Until tomorrow."

"And what do you make of that?" I asked, after our visitor had gone.

"Unless my senses are fooling me, I smell a trap," said Holmes decisively. "We have heard some strange stories in this room, old boy, but nothing quite so risible or preposterous as the one we bore witness to just now." So saying, Holmes moved swiftly to the window and stared out at the street below.

"By all that's wonderful," he cried, with great excitement. "Great Heavens, we have just been entertaining the man himself: our murderer."

I rushed to Holmes's side at the window. I saw Rubenstein clamber on to the seat of a black carriage and drive off down Baker Street.

"See, Watson, the cross in white chalk on the back of the carriage: the mark made by Wiggins before he was dislodged. We have just now encountered the man responsible for the murders of Lady Damury and Blanche Andrews, and the attempted murder of Ruth Marshall. The absolute brass nerve of the fellow!"

"What does it mean?" I asked.

"Oh, oh, that is simple enough. He hopes to lure me to that address and do away with me, of course." To my surprise Holmes gave one of his shrill, unnerving laughs. "My involvement in the case has unnerved him sufficiently to lure him out of the shadows. I must have got deep under the fellow's skin if he risked exposure by coming here to set his lure. No doubt he received some kind of thrill at entering the den of the man he views as his deadly enemy."

"But why?"

Holmes shrugged. "As a medical man you will know that there is little reason or rhyme in a twisted mind. The fellow is obviously an obsessive and I have become his obsession. He will not rest until he has killed me."

I shuddered at the thought. "What will you do?"

Chapter Twenty-four

Gustav Caligari grinned all the way back to his house in Kensington. He deemed his visit to Sherlock Holmes a tremendous success. He was sure that his story had created the desired effect, that the flimsy nature of his tale of the insomniac strangler would intrigue Holmes. He knew the man was arrogant enough not to resist the challenge he had presented. The reference to the Paddington strangling added yet more finesse to the ruse. He knew too that the suspicious nature of the scenario was the irresistible bait which would lead to the detective's downfall. Caligari was confident concerning what the great Sherlock Holmes would do next, and he would be ready for him.

On arriving home, he made his way up to Robert's room, rousing him in order to recount his adventures in Baker Street. Narrating them rather like a father telling a bedtime story to a child, Caligari gave Robert a detailed account of his interview with Holmes, adding various asides to illustrate his brilliance and skill at drawing Holmes like a fly into his sticky web.

"Of course, my dear Robert, you will play a major role in the next sequence of my plan – my plan to destroy Sherlock Holmes."

Robert stared straight ahead. Now that his feelings had atrophied, he was incapable of registering any sense of emotion on his pale ghost of a face; yet Caligari knew that he listened and understood.

Chapter Twenty-five

From the journal of Dr. John H. Watson

"A spot of burglary is in order," said Holmes with great enthusiasm.

My friend elaborated. "Rubenstein, as we must refer to him, although certainly it is not his real name, believes that I will turn up at his consulting room tomorrow just before four-thirty. He hopes to trap me and then, no doubt, attempt to kill me. So, we must be ahead of the game and break into the premises tonight to see what information we can glean, which will lead us straight to our man. He will not be expecting such an early visitation."

"Why not simply pass the matter over to the police?" I asked.

Holmes gave me a tight, sardonic grin. "I doubt if any other women are at risk. Besides, this is a personal challenge for me – I cannot refrain from accepting it. As you well know, danger is part of my trade."

"At least have Lestrade provide some support."

Holmes raised an eyebrow. "And have our quarry alerted by heavy-footed policemen?"

"Then you will not go alone," I said.

Holmes gave me a warm smile. "I have no intention of press-ganging you into this venture, my dear Watson. However, if you insist on accompanying me, I shall certainly place no obstacles in your way."

I laughed. "You will not be surprised when I state categorically that I do insist."

"The old campaigner lives! In that case, I suggest that you make sure you have your pistol with you. An Ely No. 2 is an excellent companion when one is dealing with a character who goes around strangling young women."

It was approaching midnight when we turned off the busy and brightly illuminated Marylebone High Street into Cedar Court. Along the narrow lane, crowded with small business properties, we soon found number 7, which bore a makeshift sign outside stating that this was the surgery of "Dr. A. Rubenstein". Holmes had little difficulty in forcing the feeble lock. With the aid of a pocket lantern to light our way, we entered the premises. The place smelt damp and musty. A corridor led to a flight of stairs to the upper floor and to two doors on the right-hand side, which appeared to be the extent of the downstairs area.

"As I suspected," said Holmes quietly, "the property has not been used as any kind of doctor's surgery. It has merely been rented for the purposes of a trap."

"It all seems somewhat blatant, Holmes," I said. "He had no hope of fooling you once you had stepped over the threshold of this place."

"You are quite correct. It is a fact that concerns me greatly..."

Holmes had only just uttered the words when we heard a noise in the room immediately to our right. Holmes placed his gloved finger to his lips and then, slipping his revolver from his coat pocket, pushed the door ajar with his foot.

I stood immediately behind him and, in the dim beam of the pocket lantern, observed a dark shape at the far side of the room.

"Stay where you are. I am armed," said Holmes, training the lantern onto the face of the vague figure. It was Alexander Rubenstein.

"Good evening. Why, Mr. Holmes, you are far too early for your appointment," he said smoothly and then looked away from my friend, into the shadows. "Now, Robert," he cried suddenly.

It was only then that I realised there was yet another presence in the room. A tall, dark figure emerged from the shadows near the door and struck Sherlock Holmes on the back of the head with some implement. My friend slumped to the floor, the lantern falling from his grasp, and the light went out.

"And again, Robert," came Rubenstein's voice once more. Before I knew what was happening my revolver had been knocked from my grasp and I felt cold fingers at my throat. I struggled to pull free but it was to no avail. My assailant's grip was too strong and I could feel my body growing limp as consciousness drained from me. The last thing I remember before darkness overcame me was Rubenstein's voice. "Gently, Robert. Gently," it said.

Chapter Twenty-six

Sherlock Holmes awoke with a start. He was cold and his head throbbed. It took him some moments to realise where he was and what had happened to him. With a determined focus he pulled himself up into a sitting position and tried to assemble his thoughts, which were still somewhat blurred. He had been struck a blow on the back of the head; the small egg-like lump bore witness to that. Thankfully, it felt as though the skin had not been broken. Holmes remembered seeing Rubenstein in the room, but it was not he who had attacked him – attacked him from behind. Then, as clarity grew in his mind, a worrying thought came to him: where was Watson? He gazed around the gloomy chamber but there was no sign of his friend. Had he been bludgeoned also? If so, where was he now?

He called out Watson's name but his voice merely echoed and faded in the gloom. There was no response. *If that fiend Rubenstein has harmed Watson,* he thought, the flame of anger igniting within him, *he will pay dearly for it.* He rose to his feet and dusted down his clothes. By the light of dawn, squeezing its way through the gaps in the curtains, he was able to observe footprints in the dust, but they revealed no clear scenario. What he saw, too, was a long cream envelope on the floor, a few feet from where he had lain. It bore his name on the front and he recognised the florid handwriting, which was the same as that on the note that had been left on Blanche Andrews' body. *More games*, he thought, as he tore back the flap and extracted a sheet of stiff notepaper. He read the message it contained:

> Dear Mr. Holmes
>
> The game is afoot. I present you with a little challenge. You have until midnight to discover the whereabouts of Dr. Watson. If you fail – he will die. It is as simple as that.
>
> Happy hunting.
>
> A friend.

On returning to Baker Street, his head still sore from the blow, Holmes first made a call on Mrs. Hudson to enquire about Ruth Marshall. "She's fine, if a little frustrated with looking at the four walls of her bedroom for most of the day," the landlady informed him. "She knows that her confinement is in her best interests, but that does not help matters. Mr. Firbank called yesterday, wanting to take her for a walk in the park, but I put my foot down as instructed. He was not amused at my intransigence." Her face flickered briefly into a smile. "But he is too much of a gentleman to protest."

"You are an excellent keeper of the gate. I beg that you do not weaken. There is a creature out there bent on ending this young lady's life, I assure you."

"I shall do my best, Mr. Holmes."

"Thank you. You always do, in all things. I know that I can rely on you. Have you seen Dr. Watson this morning, by chance?"

Mrs. Hudson shook her head. "No, not at all."

Holmes gave a friendly nod and left without another word. He made his way to his room, where he hurriedly washed, shaved and changed his clothes. He then sat by the empty grate and smoked a pipe of strong tobacco while he focused his mind on the problem before him, exerting the full power of his brain: what game was Rubenstein playing, and where was Watson? He was well aware that his friend was incidental to the villain's plans. The real target was himself. Rubenstein wanted to traumatise the detective before finally doing away with him. That did not unduly concern Holmes; his real worry was for Watson. A knot of fear began to harden in his chest. If any real harm came to his friend, he could never forgive himself. It was a delicate matter that should be handled with the utmost care. Holmes knew he must not involve the police. He could not trust Lestrade and his cronies to deal with the situation effectively. This was his personal challenge.

He puffed heavily on his pipe, his head enveloped in a cloud of pungent grey smoke as he struggled to out-think Rubenstein and to construct a plan of action. In his mind, he ran through their visit to the darkened house in Cedar Court. He envisioned himself and Watson at a distance, as if the two of them were characters in a play. He saw them venture into the darkened chamber on the right and the beam of his pocket lantern picking out the figure at the far side of the room. As the light sought out the man's face, it became apparent that it was Rubenstein. There was no mistaking that large face and piercing eyes. He said "Good evening," as though encountering them at some social gathering, and added in a more strident tone, "Now, Robert." This, pondered Holmes, was a command, an instruction to some other individual who had been primed for action. Then Holmes remembered the rustling sound behind him and the sudden pain he felt as he received a blow to the head. He had fallen to the floor. Heavily concussed but not yet unconscious, from ground level he was still able to register in a hazy fashion the events that occurred in the gloom around him.

Holmes sat back in his chair and closed his eyes, urging his mind to recall his last waking moments. He heard Rubenstein's voice once more: "Again, Robert." The voice was firm and commanding. Holmes felt a tingle ripple down his spine as he saw the other figure in the room make his way towards Watson. He was tall and menacing, his movements like those of a man walking in his sleep: slow, mechanical. He was responding to Rubenstein's orders as he grasped Watson by the neck and began to throttle him. It was at this point that Holmes blacked out.

His eyes sprang open, wild with excitement. *Great Heavens,* he thought, *that man who attacked Watson was hypnotised... hypnotised to carry out a violent act.*

Within minutes Sherlock Holmes was out on Baker Street hailing a cab.

Professor Christopher Clark appeared very surprised to see Holmes in his laboratory at St Mary Bethlehem Hospital once more.

"This is an unexpected pleasure," he said awkwardly.

"I am sorry to disturb you by arriving unannounced, but the matter is most urgent and I believe you may be able to help me."

"Of course. I am more than happy to assist if I can," said the professor, snapping off his rimmed glasses and cleaning them with a florid handkerchief.

"When we met before you mentioned that a burgeoning number of fake hypnotists are now practising in London – both as music-hall acts and as pseudo-consultants to the wealthy."

"Indeed. Their growing presence undermines the scientific reputation of hypnotism. If I had my way, these charlatans would be banned from carrying out their dubious services."

"Are you familiar with any of these individuals in particular?"

Absentmindedly, Clark picked up a test tube and turned it around in his thick fingers. "None personally. They are legion. I have read about a few and in my researches I have encountered one or two individuals who have been patients of these creatures. Their concern is money, not medicine."

"I am trying to locate one such individual whom I believe can help me with my enquiries."

"What is his name?"

"I am not sure. He has been using the name Rubenstein, but I fear that is an alias. He is obviously of foreign extraction: middle European. He is a tall, well-built man with short-cropped hair."

The professor shook his head. "I cannot say I know of the fellow. The real villain in this pseudo-profession, to my mind, is a character who goes by the name of Sylvester Spedding. He has been a trickster all his life, working his way up from the fairgrounds with the three-card trick to masquerading as a medium, pretending to bring people back from the dead to chat to their grieving relatives. Now he has moved on to hypnotism. It is easier to fool the public with this than with his other nefarious gimmicks and certainly it is more financially rewarding. He has a very comfy practice in smart premises in Chelsea. Really come up in the world, has Mr. Spedding."

Chapter Twenty-seven

From the journal of Dr. John H. Watson

When I finally managed to drag myself awake, I discovered that I was bound very firmly to a chair in what seemed to be a dank cellar. The only light was from an oil lamp placed on a wooden crate by the door. The walls were damp with moisture and glittered green with mould. I was conscious of scampering noises in the gloom, suggesting that mice and rats were also in residence. It took me some moments to orientate myself. I was obviously a prisoner of Alexander Rubenstein and his strange accomplice, the curious figure who had nearly throttled the life out of me. Why they had not killed me, I did not know. I wondered what fate had befallen my friend, Sherlock Holmes. I had seen him attacked and slump to the floor in that house in Cedar Court. Was he being held prisoner in some other place or, God forbid, had these villains ended his life? The thought of this filled me with dread. The possibility of losing my friend was too painful to contemplate and I banished the idea from my mind. Surely he was alive.

I was cold, hungry and mightily dismayed. I had to escape this seedy dungeon. In desperation I tugged at my bindings, but with no result. They were tight and strong, resisting all my efforts to loosen them. I gave a moan of despair before trying to rally my spirits. I was alive – for the moment. I told myself that I must not give up hope, although at present I had no foundations on which to build such a premise.

The thought occurred to me that maybe I had been left here to die, gradually to fade and rot amongst the company of rodents who, in time, would nibble at my decaying flesh. At the thought, a fresh wave of despair crashed over my troubled soul. Another session of tugging at my bonds ended as before and so, in desperation, I began to call out for help. My throat was still sore from the assault of the previous night and my voice emerged as a raw croak. I tried again and again, increasing my volume with each attempt.

I heard a noise beyond the door. It sounded like footsteps on stone stairs. After a pause, the door creaked open and there stood Alexander Rubenstein, a broad smile on his damp features.

"Ah, Doctor, you are awake at last. Good morning to you. I hope you slept well."

"Release me at once," I retorted firmly.

Rubenstein shook his head. "Tut, tut, Doctor, you know very well I cannot do that. I could not have you running off to the police, making all kinds of wild accusations against me. No, I'm afraid you will have to stay exactly where you are – for the time being, at least. But I shall have a treat for you later."

There were many utterances and oaths on the tip of my tongue but I knew that whatever I said, it would have no effect on my situation, or on the behaviour of this demented villain. I tried a different approach.

"Where is Holmes?" I asked, hoping that the question would prompt the fellow to reveal boastfully the fate of my friend.

"Where is he, indeed? Running around in circles, I imagine. Desperate to find you."

At least this puzzling response seemed to indicate that Holmes was still alive and at liberty. Perhaps by some miracle he had escaped Rubenstein's clutches. Whatever the explanation, with Holmes free there was some kind of hope.

"What are you going to do with me?" I asked, trying to keep my tone reasonable. I knew anger and brusqueness would only bring down his mental shutters.

"All in good time, Dr. Watson. I like to spring surprises on my guests and you are certainly in for a surprise. Now I suggest that you sit quietly and wait. If you begin calling out again, I am afraid I shall have to gag your mouth, which would be most uncomfortable for you."

Flashing me a most unpleasant smile, he disappeared from the chamber leaving me with my own desperate thoughts. There was nothing I could do. I had to put all my hope and faith in Sherlock Holmes.

Chapter Twenty-eight

On encountering Sylvester Spedding for the first time, Sherlock Holmes estimated him to be a cross between a pantomime villain and a racecourse tout. He had a chirpy Cockney accent, eyes that could not be trusted and a damp handshake. He was attired in rich, extravagant clothes, which looked ill at ease on his lithe yet scrawny body.

However, when Holmes called at his consulting room in a smart street in Chelsea, he had great difficulty gaining access to the great man. The receptionist, an epicene young fellow with a mop of dyed yellow hair, informed him that Mr. Spedding saw no one without a prior engagement and that his appointment book was full for at least a month. It was only when Holmes flourished a shiny sovereign and placed it on the desk within the youth's reach that his resolve finally weakened.

"I think your master will find it quite beneficial to see me now," he assured the upstart receptionist, who snatched up the sovereign in a trice before quickly disappearing into the inner sanctum. He emerged a few minutes later a different man. He wore a broad smile on his lips and affected a gracious demeanour to accompany it.

"You are most fortunate, sir," he said, his eyes twinkling merrily. "Mr. Spedding has agreed to see you. If you would care to step this way." He flung open the double doors and made a dramatic bowing gesture to usher Holmes inside.

The room was opulent and garish. Colours clashed and artworks of dubious quality cluttered the walls. Vibrant curtains cascaded from the solitary window and one corner of the room was a virtual jungle of ferns. A lurid green velvet chaise longue was placed before an ugly ornate mahogany desk. *A great deal of money has been spent on these furnishings*, thought Holmes. *A great deal of money, but no taste.*

Seated behind the grotesquely carved desk was the man Holmes had come to see. As Holmes approached, Spedding rose from his chair and threw out his right hand.

"Pleased to meet you, sir, I'm sure."

By his tone and phrasing, Holmes placed the fellow as a son of the slums of Bethnal Green. As Professor Clark had observed, he had "come up in the world".

Sherlock Holmes took the pale, bony paw that was offered to him and shook it. He noticed that Spedding was clutching the sovereign in his other hand.

"Thank you for seeing me," Holmes said.

My pleasure, Mr...?"

"Watson. John Watson."

Spedding nodded and jotted the name down on a sheet of paper on his desk. "I must inform you that consultations are five guineas a session," he said, throwing Holmes a practised beatific smile. "I shall require payment before we can continue." His manner was pleasant but avarice gleamed in his eyes.

Holmes nodded and proceeded to count out further coins. He handed them over and Spedding collected them up greedily before slipping them into the desk drawer. He sat down again and leaned towards his new client, a broad grin on his face which revealed two gold teeth glinting in the harsh light.

"Do take a seat," he said, and Holmes obeyed, perching awkwardly on the edge of the chaise longue. He had no intention of lying upon it like a patient in readiness to be hypnotised.

"Now then, Mr. Watson, down to business. What is your concern? What is it that troubles you?"

"I am not here to see you for treatment, Mr. Spedding. I seek information."

Spedding's smile, along with the gold teeth, disappeared in an instant. "Information? I'm afraid I don't understand."

"You are very successful in your... profession, I believe."

The smile returned. "I certainly am. One doesn't get a gaff like this" – he raised his arm in praise of the room – "by not being top nob in your game. I have a duke and a knight what are clients of mine."

"Quite. But is it not true that the competition in your line of work is growing? More and more hypnotherapists are setting up practices in London almost daily."

Spedding nodded his head vigorously. "You are quite correct, sir. A lot of sham devils are polluting the stream. Shysters and charlatans they are, the lot of them. A true hypnotist is a gifted individual with a God-given talent. We are legitimate practitioners of hypnotherapeutic healing. We are not a quack, out to make some easy money like so many of these imposters."

"I do so agree with you," said Holmes warmly. "And that is why I am desirous of tracking down one such imposter who has done a friend of mine a great disservice. Unfortunately I do not know the fellow's name. I assumed that you, at the peak of the profession, would be aware of all such false practitioners."

Spedding's eyes widened with enthusiasm. "Most likely. I like to keep my finger on the pulse, as it were. The more of these bleedin' charlatans set up in business, the more my profits are in jeopardy. Who is this creature that you want to track down?"

"He is a foreigner. A big man with heavy features and short-cropped hair. Tends to wear a coat with a fur collar and a homburg hat."

Spedding pulled a sour face. "Oh, you must mean Caligari. Your description fits that bounder exactly. He has only recently appeared on the scene – a year ago maybe – but he has managed to wheedle his way into attending top-notch parties, where he fools silly society women with his promises, convincing them that he can rid them of their petty little foibles."

Much as you do, thought Holmes. "What can you tell me about this Caligari?"

Spedding shrugged his inadequate shoulders. "I can tell you he's a bloody nuisance. I've lost clients to him. I don't know where he come from; I only know I wish he'd go back there. I know nothing of his background."

"Where does he practise?"

"He has his consulting rooms in Kensington. Sedgwick Street, I believe."

"Do you know if he has a partner? A tall fellow?"

"Not as far as I know. He treads the wire as a solo artist. What's this trouble he's in with your friend?"

"I am afraid I cannot divulge that," said Holmes smoothly, rising from the chaise longue. "I promised I would treat the matter with discretion. I am sure you understand. However, I thank you very much for the information you have provided. It has been most useful."

Spedding threw up his hands in a casual gesture. "Any time, Mr. Watson. It's been a pleasure to do business with you." As he said this, he could not resist casting a glance at the drawer in his desk where the five guineas resided and once more, his eyes lit up with avaricious pleasure.

It is, mused Holmes, as he left the premises, *the most money I have ever parted with to gain a slender piece of information, but nevertheless it is vital if I am to save Watson.*

Chapter Twenty-nine

℃

From the journal of Dr. John H. Watson

"You are feeling tired, eh?"

The voice broke into my consciousness and prompted me to raise my head. I realised that despite my perilous situation, fatigue had overtaken me and I had fallen asleep. In an instant, I shook away the cobwebs of slumber and recalled my circumstances, which remained the same. I was still tightly bound to the chair in the dingy cellar of some unknown building. I was still a prisoner of Rubenstein. The man himself stood before me, the usual mocking, oleaginous grin on his face. Oh, how I wished I could remove that smirk – preferably with a firm uppercut to the jaw. Such desires, however, were impotent. Secured firmly to the chair, I was like a paralysed man.

"Sleep is a great healer, is it not?" he said smoothly. "I recall what your great playwright had to say on the matter in his play *Macbeth*: 'Sleep that knits up the ravelled sleeve of care, The death of each day's life, sore labour's bath, Balm of hurt minds, great nature's second course'. So beautiful, isn't it? So apt. Sleep is so powerful, you know, Dr. Watson. Once it overtakes the brain, self-will, rationality and even morality fall into a neutral mode. I am sure you have yourself experienced dreams in which you have behaved in a manner that is totally at odds with your waking self. That is quite natural. You would not be human if you did otherwise, I assure you. Once released from the restraints of consciousness and all the considerations that they impose, the brain is free and unfettered. I know because I have studied and explored the phenomenon. You see, I am a mesmerist, a hypnotherapist. Do you know what that is?"

"Yes," I said coldly. "I know what you are," I added with a sneer.

"With my skills in hypnosis I have control. Indeed I have the power over life and death."

"Why would anyone want such an awesome responsibility?"

Rubenstein grinned. "Such power creates freedom – the ultimate autonomy. And it brings me pleasure. It elevates me above the norm, the insects of the world, the rabble."

"Have you ever considered that you may well be mad?"

Now the fiend laughed out loud. "What a simple mind you have, Doctor. Through the ages such accusations have been levelled at all those who have risen above the throng, those with vision and the ability to develop a power to create their own path through life. To their blind critics – to people like you with restricted vision – that may seem a kind of madness, but to me it is a serene and magnificent sanity. You are the insane one, running around ant-like in your drab little fashion, meekly accepting the assaults of life's slings and arrows rather than taking pains to rise above them, to take control of your own destiny. As a result, I wear the crown and you squirm about in the mud."

"There is no crown to be worn by a common murderer –

someone who in a cowardly fashion snuffs out the life of innocent people."

"You see, you make my point for me. That is your narrow, simple myopic view of the matter. I am as a god-like surgeon, who stands over the body of my patient with the ability to save or end life. I simply choose the latter. That is what brings me the greatest happiness."

I gazed at this demon, his moist skin shining in the dim light, teeth exposed in a chilling grin and eyes wide with unstable excitement. I have never been more convinced in my life that I was in the presence of a maniac.

"So," I responded calmly, "now you intend to kill me to satisfy what you regard as some intellectual bloodlust."

Rubenstein pursed his lips. "Oh, Dr. Watson, you certainly have a way with words, but they are empty of force and meaning. If they are meant to wound or incense me, they fail miserably. They are blunt arrows wide of their target. Am I going to kill you? Eventually. But before I take you to that particular brink, I have a task for you. I require your assistance. You see, when I latch on to an idea I follow it to the end, never wavering in my determination to see it to a successful conclusion."

"I will walk across the fires of Hell barefoot before I help you," I cried, with great passion.

My outburst amused Rubenstein greatly. He gave a gentle chuckle before responding. "I don't think that you will have any choice in the matter, my friend. It seems that you have not been paying full attention. You are hardly in a position to refuse."

He paused for a moment as if a thought had struck him. "Let me explain the matter to you, Doctor. I have to admit that from time to time I do, as you English say, get a bee in my bonnet. Something that irritates me to such an extent that I become very focused in my anger, determined to eradicate that particular bee – squash it until the bodily juices spill out. At the moment your annoying colleague Sherlock Holmes is that buzzing creature, and I intend to destroy him. To squash him underfoot. He foiled my plans, you see. Prevented me from eliminating the Marshall girl. That upset me greatly. I cannot forgive him for it. And so all my energies now are spent on my revenge. First he must suffer and then he will die. I have already given him pain and distress by kidnapping you. No doubt at this very moment, he is running around London trying to follow up clues in order to discover where you are. Don't worry, he will succeed. I have confidence in him. After all, he is the Great Detective. He will, I am sure, track you down. And in doing so, track me down. And we will be ready for him, won't we, Dr. Watson? Primed and ready."

"I don't know what on earth you are babbling on about, Rubenstein," I said as casually as I could, despite the knot of fear that was beginning to form in my stomach.

"Rubenstein? Oh, I am not Rubenstein. I am Caligari. Caligari, the master hypnotist." He suddenly moved towards me with a darting motion and ripped back the sleeve of my shirt, exposing my right arm. "For the moment, I need to raise the veil from your eyes regarding your friend Mr. Sherlock Holmes. You will assist me in this matter."

"Never. I would rather die."

He chuckled softly and retreated to the far corner of the room, returning seconds later carrying a hypodermic needle.

"Time to knit up that ravelled sleeve of care," he observed as he inserted the needle into my naked arm and pressed down on the piston. "There now. That will help you relax."

"Whatever you do to me, you will not succeed in getting the upper hand on Sherlock Holmes."

"What a naïve fellow you are, Watson."

It took but a few moments for the wretched drug to have an effect on me. I was consumed with an almost overpowering sense of tiredness, my body growing limp and my vision blurring, as though I were viewing the world through frosted glass. But the overall sensation was that of ease. I no longer held any worries or dark concerns regarding my situation. Indeed, I found myself smiling.

Chapter Thirty

Caligari watched with great satisfaction as the drug took hold of Watson. His body relaxed and his head slipped downwards gently, as though he had lost the use of the muscles in his neck. But the eyes, though glazed, remained open.

"Welcome to my world, Dr. Watson. The little drug I have just administered will help you come around to my way of thinking. To begin with, I want to find out about your friendship with Sherlock Holmes. I have studied all the published accounts of your investigations with him. He is a good friend to you?"

Watson did not respond immediately. His mind was too fogged by the drug to provide an instant response. At length he raised his head a little and repeated: "He is a good friend."

"He never lets you down... this paragon?"

"Never."

"Ah, I think that is not true. Does he not sometimes disappoint you? Take you for granted?"

Again, there was a pause before Watson responded. "I do

not mind. It is simply his way."

"You do not mind? Even when he implies that you are somewhat... stupid?"

"He has never done that."

Caligari chuckled. "Oh, come now. You are not only trying to fool me, but yourself. I know that on several occasions he has called your perceptions, your intelligence, into question. Did he not once observe that you are not particularly luminous..."

"By comparison with Holmes I am not..."

"And he has certainly pushed that point home on many occasions, has he not?"

Watson made no reply.

"Time to delve a little deeper, I think," said Caligari. "Time to make you see how obnoxious this man is." He reached into his waistcoat pocket and produced a gold watch, holding it before his victim's bemused face and beginning to swing it to and fro.

"I want you to sleep now, Watson. Allow your mind to be free of all constraints. You will listen to me and absorb my instructions, my statements, as though they were your own. You will think like me. Is that understood?"

Again there was a long pause and Caligari realised that Watson was struggling to respond. He was fighting against the effect of the drug and the hypnotic passes – but it was a losing battle.

"Do not fight it, Doctor. Relax and surrender to my will. See the watch: how charming it is. Swinging to and fro. It helps to release the shackles on your mind. You are now free to accept new thoughts. New beliefs. My thoughts and my beliefs. You will think like me. Isn't that so?"

Watson's eyes followed the trajectory of the swinging timepiece and then his dry lips trembled for a moment as he spoke in a faint, hoarse whisper: "Yes."

Caligari beamed. "Good. Now you are completely, totally under my influence. It is time to tell you what a despicable character your so-called friend is. How he has abused your good nature, tricked you and treated you like a fool. You know how the world sees you, thanks to Mr. Sherlock Holmes. You are his puppet, a menial employed to polish his ego. He has no respect for you. Remember the Baskerville case, how he kept you in the dark all that time. He treated you like a dolt. He did not trust you. He did not respect your intellect."

"He did. He does trust me, respect me," Watson whispered slowly, his eyelids flickering, fingers trying and failing to grasp at anything that might pull him from this nightmarish loss of control. But it was hopeless. He felt himself sinking deeper into oblivion.

"Oh, but he did not," murmured Caligari, irked by his subject's ability to fight the drug. He was confident, however, that his expertise would prevail, although perhaps a slightly higher dose of the drug would assist. He prepared a second hypodermic, smiling as he injected another vein firmly. Watson winced and his eyelids flickered erratically.

"Now, where were we? Your friend Mr. Sherlock Holmes, hmm? He neither trusts nor respects you. He despises you."

"Trust. Respect..." murmured Watson in soft guttural tones.

"By return, why should you trust and respect him, the man who laughs at your efforts to help him? How often has he made you feel small and insignificant? How often has he told you that you have failed?"

"Failed."

"Many times."

"Yes... many times."

"He let you mourn him for many months when you thought him dead, drowned in that waterfall in Switzerland. He has no consideration for your feelings. He treats you badly because he sees you as incompetent, Watson. You are dull and stupid."

Watson shook his head. "He shouldn't have done that. He didn't mean to but it was cruel."

"Cruel, indeed. Sherlock Holmes is cruel. Now we are getting somewhere."

Some long and frustrating hours later Caligari sat in the gloom of the cellar smoking a cigar, an expression of deep satisfaction on his face. He glanced over at the now-unconscious Watson and grinned. It had not been easy, and had taken several attempts to fracture Watson's instinctive and annoyingly deep core of admiration for the damned detective, but in the end Caligari's efforts had borne fruit. Watson was now his. He had broken down his victim's great core of love for Holmes. The effect of the drug and his mastery of the hypnotic technique had corrupted Watson's mind. The doctor was now his puppet, his instrument, one that would bring about the destruction of Mr. Sherlock Holmes.

Chapter Thirty-one

℘

Sherlock Holmes stood in the shadows on the far side of the road, gazing at the property opposite. It was 34 Sedgwick Street, Kensington, the designated address of Gustav Caligari, hypnotherapist.

This, thought Holmes, was where the trail ended. Or, he hoped that it was where the trail ended. He was convinced that he was correct in his belief that Alexander Rubenstein was really Gustav Caligari and, for some perverted motive, had taken Watson to use as bait to lure him to this address. All the clues were present and he well knew the way that the mind of a monomaniac functioned. The fact that Caligari had not killed him when he had been rendered unconscious in the empty premises in Cedar Court – the perfect opportunity to do so – clearly indicated the unstable nature of the man's mind. It was as though he wished to play a game of cat and mouse in order to extend the control he possessed as a hypnotist. He had already exerted the ultimate power by dealing in death. He was responsible for the demise of two women already – he and his strange accomplice. A vision of the tall, stiff-legged figure in the darkened room came to his mind. The vivid memory confirmed his theory that this odd creature was in thrall to Caligari's powers of hypnotism. He was, in fact, his instrument of death.

As Holmes observed the building across the road, he lit a cigarette and considered his options. Were Caligari and his strange partner inside just waiting for him to arrive, to ride to Watson's rescue? Waiting, in readiness, so they could kill him and Watson together? Or was this another trick? Would he find the place deserted? Would there be another cream envelope awaiting him with another taunting message? These were questions he simply could not answer. One thing was certain. This was his challenge. He could trust no one else with the task. If necessary the police would clean up the mess afterwards. For now, he had no option but to go in there and find out.

He had decided that he would not attempt an illegal entry, clambering in through a window at the rear or any other such melodramatic activity. He would enter by way of the front door. There were moments in his career when he had put all thoughts of his personal safety to one side in order to secure a successful outcome. These had been effective so far, but each had presented him with a dangerous challenge and maybe one day he would fail. Yet, he reasoned, this was a crucial aspect of his calling as a detective, one he could neither deny nor avoid. How could he shy away from the task when the safety of his dear friend was at stake? With a determined shrug of the shoulders, he threw his cigarette in the gutter and crossed the road.

He stood before the door for a few moments before taking any action. Rather than ring the bell, he turned the handle, and within moments he was standing in a small, dimly lit hallway. He withdrew his pistol, but before he was able to take another step forward, he heard a voice ring out: "In here, Mr. Holmes. The room to your right."

It was Caligari.

Holmes approached and opened the door swiftly, letting it swing back firmly against the wall in order to ensure no one was hiding there. He quickly surveyed the room. No lamp or fire was lit and pools of gloom lay in wait in the corners. The room was sparsely furnished with a few chairs, a small side table, a chaise longue and, by the window, a monstrous leafy aspidistra, its dark leaves resting against the drawn blind, casting abstract, jagged shadows across the room from the streetlamp outside. In the centre of the room was a desk, behind which was seated Gustav Caligari.

His bulk lay in blackest shadow, but Holmes could see from a brief glint that a shark-like smile had flitted across the face of the hypnotist.

"What a dramatic entrance, Mr. Holmes. And carrying a gun also. My, my. You appear like a furtive criminal rather than the revered upholder of the law that you profess yourself to be. Do you intend to shoot me?"

"That is not beyond the bounds of possibility," replied Holmes smoothly, his impressive dark brow set in a fierce frown. Slowly he took a step closer to Caligari, after scanning his surroundings to make sure that no other persons were present.

"Then this may prove to be a very entertaining interview. You will not be surprised to learn that I too have a weapon." He raised his right hand above the desk to reveal that he was holding a pistol. "I do hope that the police do not arrive here some time later to find two bodies on the floor. It would be such a loss to mankind for us to shoot one another."

"Where is Watson?"

"Ah, yes, Watson. Good old Watson. You are missing your friend, no doubt. I am aware of how much you mean to each other."

"I will ask you one more time. Where is he?" Holmes said, his voice cold and harsh, eyes glittering with suppressed anger.

"You would like to see him, no doubt. Very well, I have no wish to disappoint you. I will arrange for him to visit us."

Caligari placed the gun on the desk and retrieved a small silver whistle from his waistcoat pocket. With great deliberation, he placed it in his mouth and blew. A thin, reedy, high-pitched sound emerged, echoing eerily around the room.

As though in response to the whistle, there were sudden noises outside the room: a door opening and footsteps approaching. Holmes turned slightly and saw Watson standing in the doorway, haggard face coated with perspiration and shoulders stooped as though supporting an invisible heavy burden. But it was the eyes that fascinated and shocked Holmes. No longer the lively intelligent eyes of his old friend, they were like the blue empty shells of a dead man. It was almost as though he were sightless. So odd and disturbing was his appearance that Holmes took a step back.

"Now," cried Caligari.

At the sound of his voice, Watson's eyes flickered more brightly, focusing on Holmes. Before the detective could react, his friend approached him and aimed a savage blow at the hand holding the pistol. The impact was so powerful that Holmes involuntarily released his grip on the weapon and it went spinning across the room into the far corner.

In the next instant, Watson leapt forward and grabbed Holmes around the throat in a tight stranglehold. Holmes tried to fight back, pushing hard against Watson's chest, but he struggled in vain.

It was though his friend were imbued with the strength of two men. As the grip around his neck grew tighter, he was driven towards the desk. He gasped for air, realising at last that this creature was no longer Watson, his old friend and companion. He had been turned into a murderous automaton through Caligari's power of hypnotism – with the aid, he suspected, of some powerful narcotic cocktail designed to suppress free will and which appeared to provide him with an almost inhuman energy.

Watson rammed Holmes against the desk, forcing him backwards and down onto its surface, all the while maintaining the iron grip on his erstwhile companion's throat. Holmes was aware of Caligari slipping from his chair and moving out of range of the confrontation. He knew that only a few moments of consciousness remained to him as Watson squeezed the air out of his lungs. His hands flailed along the desk, searching for an object he had observed when he first entered the room. At last his fingers found it, and with a great effort he was able to snatch hold of the glass paperweight. He swung it up, hard, against Watson's forehead. The result was instantaneous. Watson cried out in pain and immediately his fingers relaxed their hold. Within seconds the detective pushed his assailant away. Watson staggered backwards, his eyes blinking wildly before they focused on Holmes. "My God," he croaked, his right arm shooting out, pointing at his friend. "My God," he repeated. "Holmes, what..." Words failed him and he sank to the floor in a swoon, a minute trickle of blood running down his forehead from the wound made by the paperweight.

A shot rang out and Holmes felt the bullet whistle by his ear. He dropped to the floor and, with a few deft movements, stretched out his arm and managed to retrieve his own gun. Caligari fired again and missed, but this time Holmes returned fire.

From the darkness there emerged an agonised cry and two furious dark eyes glittered in the shadows, indicating that Holmes had been more successful in his aim.

"That's for Watson!" Holmes cried, staggering towards Caligari.

The hypnotist's fierce features crumpled with pain and he made towards the door, now desperate to escape. Holmes fired once more but this time, in the darkness, the bullet struck only the panel of the closing door.

Stopping to bend over Watson, Holmes checked that his friend was breathing normally. He was, he deduced, suffering from a mild concussion. Satisfied at his diagnosis, and trembling with rage, Holmes sped after Caligari.

From the sound of the fleeting footsteps from the upper floor, it was clear that Caligari was making his way to the top of the house rather than out into the street, where it would be easy to lose himself in the maze of thoroughfares that the city had to offer. This alarmed Holmes somewhat, but he did not delay in racing up the steps in hot pursuit. As he approached the stairway to the third landing, all sounds had ceased, and an uneasy silence settled on the premises. Crouching down, he made his way cautiously up towards the top landing. Like a hunter, he cocked his head and listened for some sign of his prey. There was a sound, a kind of faint rustling, its precise nature indistinct.

Holmes moved up a step and waited before venturing further. It was then that he heard from one of the rooms the eerie whistle and Caligari's cry, "Now!" In an instant the door flew open and a tall, dark shape appeared in the aperture. Without hesitation, it began moving forward. This was the strange, shadowy individual who had attacked him in the house in Cedar Court.

With almost preternatural speed, the man was on him. "Stop or

I shoot," Holmes cried, but before he had time to aim his pistol, his attacker had grabbed him by the neck, with long firm fingers at his throat. The ferocity of the attack forced Holmes backwards and both men crashed hard against the banister. His assailant now held Holmes's arms to his sides, preventing him from raising his pistol. In desperation Holmes pulled the trigger but the bullet thudded harmlessly into the carpet. As his fingers were forced apart his grip loosened on his weapon, which fell to the floor.

Again Holmes felt long nails digging into the muscles of his neck. As his vision blurred once more, he realised that this creature was a much more accomplished assassin than Watson. He must have had more practice, no doubt. Under Caligari's orders, it was surely this fiend who had been responsible for the murders of the two women, and perhaps more. Holmes's body swayed and sagged as his limbs began to lose their power. By now, the pair were leaning over the banister rail into the dark well of the staircase.

As the creature struggled with his victim, the weight of the two bodies moving back and forth placed an excess of pressure on the brittle construction. Suddenly there was a sharp crack as a section of woodwork snapped and gave way, crashing to the ground three floors below. The man gave a startled cry of horror and immediately released his hold of the detective. Both men tried to pull back from the yawning abyss but yet tottered on the edge of the landing, each in danger of losing his balance and plunging below. Their arms flailed, grasping for an invisible hold to prevent them from tumbling to certain death.

Holmes's assailant was the first to slip over the edge. With a strangled cry, arms waving wildly, he dropped down swiftly into the maw of darkness. There was an ugly muffled thud as his body hit the floor, and Holmes too began to slide over the edge. He flung his arms out and managed to catch hold of the floorboards where the broken banister had been. His fingers barely managing to secure a tentative hold on a section of loose carpet, he hung there, swaying gently like a faulty pendulum.

He thought that if he could move his way round to grasp the remains of the banister, which were still in place, he would with its support be able to haul himself up to safety. With great effort, he stretched one hand six inches along and secured a hold, gripping the edge as tightly as he could. He was just about to reach out with the other hand when he sensed movement above him. *It must be Caligari,* he thought, and his whole body chilled at the notion. As he gazed up, he saw the hypnotist staring down at him. Although Caligari's face was in shadowy relief, Holmes could see his manic smile and the eyes that blazed with a mixture of hatred and wild delight.

"Time to say goodbye, Mr. Holmes," he said, in tones oozing with self-satisfaction. He stepped forward and placed his shoe on the fingers of Holmes's right hand. With an obscene chuckle he pressed down, hard.

The pain was excruciating and Holmes was forced to pull his hand away, leaving him hanging by one arm in space. With slow deliberation, Caligari moved to the right and placed his foot on Holmes's other hand. But before he was able to exert any pressure, his attention was diverted by a noise. He gazed over to the staircase and saw, to his great surprise, the figure of Dr. Watson, features wild and distraught, a strange zig-zag of red marking the left side of his temple where he had been wounded. "You infernal devil!" he cried and hurled a missile in the direction of Caligari. It was the desk paperweight that Holmes had used to stun him.

Watson's aim was remarkably accurate. The glass globe struck

Caligari in the middle of his forehead and with a loud, guttural croak of pain he fell backwards, hitting his head with great force on the wall as he fell. He lay still in a crumpled heap – unconscious.

Watson reached the top landing just as Holmes was trying to secure his hold again with his right hand.

"Don't worry, old fellow," cried Watson. "I have you." So saying, he leaned over and, grabbing both of Holmes's arms, pulled with all his might. It was no easy task but, gradually, he managed to haul his friend to safety, then sat down suddenly, shaking.

For a moment, Holmes lay on the landing, attempting to catch his breath. Having regained some equilibrium, he raised his head slowly, an expression of grim amusement on his face. He leaned forward and patted Watson on the back. "As I've said on many occasions, my dear Watson, I am lost without my Boswell."

Chapter Thirty-Two

From the journal of Dr. John H. Watson

Sherlock Holmes and I sat in silence for some ten minutes on the top landing of Caligari's house, collecting our thoughts and attempting to revive our shattered spirits. At length, Holmes gazed over at the still-prone figure of Caligari and gave me a nod. "We had better tie this fellow up before he regains consciousness and causes further trouble."

"Indeed," I said in firm agreement as we both scrambled to our feet. My head still throbbed, and I have no doubt Holmes's neck was raw from the assault by Caligari's puppet. Nevertheless we set about our task with some purpose. Having managed to secure some curtain cords from one of the bedrooms, we trussed Caligari up like a goose at Christmas.

We had completed our task when the villain began to rouse from his enforced slumber. There was a loud bang downstairs and we peered over the landing to the hall below. What fresh horror was this? To my profound relief, Lestrade and two constables had burst in through the front door.

"Lestrade!" cried Holmes. "You have missed the excitement, I'm afraid."

"You said to give you half an hour," the policeman replied.

"Your watch is accurate, Inspector, but thank you. It is always reassuring to have you at my back." He sighed heavily.

"Is everything all right, Mr. Holmes?"

"It is now," Holmes replied wearily. "Let's get this fellow to Scotland Yard and into a cell as quickly as possible. I shall not be content until he is behind bars."

Without undue difficulty, we managed to deliver Caligari to the Yard. On leaving the house with our prisoner, we passed the crumpled remains of his accomplice, sprawled face down in the hall, a thick pool of blood collecting around his smashed skull.

"The poor devil," said Holmes. "His eyes were completely blank – like yours, my dear Watson. It seems to me that he was merely Caligari's pawn."

"It is more like gothic fiction than real life," I observed.

Caligari offered no resistance to our efforts and remained mute on the journey. Within an hour he was incarcerated in one of the cells at Scotland Yard and we were sitting in Inspector Lestrade's office, drinking hot sweet tea as normality slowly began to seep into our tired bodies.

"Well, this is a bloomin' turn-up for the books," said Lestrade expansively, leaning back in his chair, hands behind his head. "Of course, I'll take your word for it that this fellow is a villain, and the one responsible for the deaths of Lady Damury and that other poor girl."

"And the attempted murder of Ruth Marshall... and Sherlock Holmes," I added.

"Quite. But, with due respect, I'll need more information and evidence other than your say-so. My superiors will need such stuff."

"Of course," said Holmes, somewhat wearily. "I will tell you all I know, but for a complete picture we shall have to interview the man himself. With luck, if he is malleable, he will be able to fill in the large gaps in our knowledge of this very dark affair. I suspect that he will be more than happy to regale you with all the details you need to secure his conviction. These egomaniacs are such very chatty fellows. No doubt if you search his premises you will find records of his experiments and machinations."

Lestrade gave a nod of understanding.

"May I suggest we leave that until the morning?" said Holmes. "I am feeling a little fatigued at present. I am sure a good night's sleep will help to restore my normal faculties."

"Oh, course, Mr. Holmes. You have been through a great ordeal – both you and Dr. Watson."

Holmes gave him a wintry smile. "Yes, it is not every day that your friend tries to strangle you and then saves your life." He gave a brief chuckle. "In the meantime, might I suggest you send some officers down to Sedgwick Street in Kensington and pick up the corpse of Caligari's accomplice?"

That evening Mrs. Hudson excelled herself, providing us with a hearty dinner in which a brace of pheasant proved to be the main event. However, in truth, neither Holmes nor I had much of an appetite and we did little justice to the fare on offer. We were still weary from our aches and pains, our minds awhirl with the rush of events that had occurred in the last two days. My mind was still somewhat cobwebby regarding the period when I had been drugged and hypnotised. The red marks around my friend's neck bore vivid witness to the physical traumas he had undergone.

"This has been a most unusual case," observed Holmes, pushing away his plate and lighting his pipe. "The convoluted trail we have followed is unique in my detective career. Who would have thought that the investigation of a stolen gem would lead us to a series of murders committed by a madman who used a somnambulist as his instrument of death? It resembles something from the works of Mr. Edgar Allan Poe. More fiction than fact."

"And yet it did all happen, and we have the physical scars to prove it," I added ruefully.

"Indeed. But the scars will fade in time."

"You are no doubt right," I agreed, "although I am not so sure about the dark memories. The aspect of this terrible business that horrifies me is the power that this man could exert over the mind. I have always considered myself a fellow of strong, independent thought, and yet Caligari took control of my thinking, transformed it, corrupted it. He made me truly want to kill you. He changed my whole nature. I was no longer myself. I became his creature."

"It certainly is a terrible power, but do not dwell on it, my dear Watson. You will know well from your own medical knowledge how fragile the brain is, and how events can affect one's mental outlook. You will have experienced yourself how the traumas of battle change a man's personality. Such sensitivity is what makes us human. Happily, in your case the effect was brought on by artificial means and was temporary. You must now wipe it from your memory." He leaned forward and touched me on the shoulder. "It is so comforting and reassuring to me to see you sitting across from me, restored to your old self. Fear not, Caligari's influence will not affect you again."

I gave a bleak smile. "I trust you are right."

"Neither of us must dwell on this most unsettling episode." We sat for a few moments in silence, before Holmes pulled back the chair from the table and rubbed his hands together in a business-like fashion. "However, I must say now I am eager to learn the full details behind this bizarre case. I pray that Caligari will be cooperative tomorrow and, like so many criminals when they are caught, will be more than happy to roll out all the facts in an act of self-aggrandisement."

"Let us hope so."

"Now, Watson, although the evening is young, I feel ready for my bed. A good night's sleep beckons, with the promise of a calmer dawn tomorrow."

To my chagrin, the following morning I felt worse than I had done the previous day. My energy level was very low and the pain in my head still throbbed viciously. All I wanted to do was return to my bed and sleep off my malaise.

"And so you should," said Holmes, who with his usual remarkable resilience was at the breakfast table very much his old self, tucking into scrambled eggs and toast. His eyes were bright, as was his manner. Even the marks at his throat appeared largely to have faded.

"But I do not wish to miss the interview with Caligari. I really must write it up for my notes."

"Are you really in a fit state for such a task? Is your brain functioning at its best?" He shook his head and I could not but agree. "Fear not, Watson, I shall be your eyes and ears on this occasion. Retire once more to your bed and rest, and this evening I shall recount in detail what transpired in the interview with Mr.

Caligari. You may rely on me to provide you with a full record of the proceedings."

I did not hesitate to accept his offer. I knew Holmes was right. My mind was sluggish and lacking the appropriate focus for such a task.

"Very well. A return to my bed is too tempting to resist," I said.

"A wise decision, old fellow. All will be revealed to you this evening," said Holmes brightly, buttering a second slice of toast.

I spent the rest of the day in bed, dosing myself with a strong powder for my thumping headache and crawling under the covers. It was late afternoon when I resurfaced and shook the sleep from my eyes. To my delight, I felt refreshed, and so much more alert than I had at breakfast. The onslaught of pain in my head had diminished to a minor irritation and my mind seemed clear and active. It was with some speed that I washed, dressed and made my way down to our sitting room where I found Holmes ensconced in his usual chair by the fire, puffing away on his black briar.

At my entrance he turned his head lazily in my direction. "Ah, Watson, good to see you up and about again. I refrained from waking you on my return. I thought a few more hours of slumber would do you the world of good. I can see from your flushed cheeks and bright eyes that I was right."

I nodded. "I do feel much better. More my old self."

"I am delighted. Now I am sure you are very anxious to hear my news."

"Indeed I am."

"Then if you will pour us both a small brandy, I shall give you a full recital of my adventures at Scotland Yard."

I did as requested and then sat opposite my friend in readiness.

"Lestrade took us into an interview room where the prisoner was already in situ, handcuffed, of course, with a burly constable also in attendance. Caligari seemed cheerful and almost pleased to see me. As I took a seat opposite him, he threw me a cheery smile. Here was a man ready to tell us all, to relish in his villainy. All I had to do was ask him to tell me his story – and he did."

As Holmes began his recital of his interview with Caligari, I grabbed my notebook in order to record an accurate account for my journal, which I now present here:

It was in a dank, windowless room in the basement at Scotland Yard that Holmes and Inspector Lestrade met with Caligari. He was handcuffed and accompanied by a burly, moustachioed constable.

"Welcome, gentlemen. I am so glad to see you," Caligari said in smooth arrogant tones, his eyes sparkling with dark pleasure.

"Are you ready to confess? To tell us your tale?" asked Lestrade gruffly.

"Indeed, I am eager to do so – to tell you my tale, as you put it. I am Gustav Caligari. I am the most powerful hypnotist in the world," he began. "I developed my God-given talent in my home city of Prague and when I knew that I had achieved the ultimate powers of my art, the ability to bring about death by using a subject to kill another human being, I was keen to travel to exercise my powers elsewhere. I was possessed of a long-held desire to visit Britain, and London in particular, that great progressive city swarming with a melting pot of many nationalities. Here I could build my base. Here I could kill and remain undiscovered.

"You no doubt think I am mad, or possessed by the Devil, to harbour such desires. But I tell you that you are mistaken. To have power over life and death as one wishes is surely one of mankind's ultimate aims. There is nothing new about such a desire. Cain murdered Abel and so the process began. Death is part of our existence. We all live with death. We should not shun it. It is the distant rumble of thunder at life's picnic. We ignore it at our peril. You see, I do not kill for gain, merely for the sake of scientific advancement, for pleasure, or in some instances for revenge. I wanted you dead, Mr. Holmes, because you interfered with my plans. You disturbed the smooth track of my schemes. For this I could not forgive you."

"And the women?" Holmes asked.

"Lady Damury was rude to me. She dismissed my overtures. It was unforgivable. Literally unforgivable. On the other hand, Miss Ruth Marshall was a whim. I am allowed those, you know. I was in search of a victim and my eye fell on her. I had seen her performing on stage and she attracted me. I knew instinctively that she would reject any romantic advances I made to her, and so by proxy she had dismayed me and therefore was an ideal candidate. The other woman was not only compensation for the failure with Miss Marshall but to upset your little apple cart, Mr. Holmes. You thought you had been so smart in saving the Marshall girl. I showed you I was smarter."

Holmes merely nodded. He was well aware that it would be futile to attempt to contradict this megalomaniac. Or, indeed, to interrupt him, for he was being so helpful in detailing his motives and actions that it would have been foolish to stop his flow. Instead he posed a question: "But you did not actually commit these murders yourself. You employed an accomplice."

Caligari bristled at this. "Accomplice!" he sneered. "Robert was not my accomplice. He was merely my tool, my instrument of death. He had no conscious knowledge of what he did. I controlled his thoughts, his actions, his whole being. He was my slave, mentally reliant on me."

"Who was he?" Holmes asked.

Caligari shrugged. "I have no idea. I have no notion of his history. When I first encountered him he was some kind of derelict, living on the streets. Where he came from, who he was, I have no idea. Those details did not interest me. He was vulnerable, in possession of an innate fury which had allowed him to take a life. And he was malleable."

"You kidnapped him and warped his mind."

"I trained him."

"To kill."

Caligari grinned. "Yes. To kill. To kill at my command."

"But he was not to kill Dr. Watson once you had him in your grasp," Holmes prompted.

Caligari gave another smile. "Watson was to die in due course, but in truth he was merely a pawn to snare you. And it nearly worked. What a wonderful achievement it would have been to destroy the famous Sherlock Holmes and his biographer in one fell swoop. Well, maybe next time."

At this point Lestrade leaned forward, wagging his finger. "There won't be a next time for you, my lad. It's the gallows for you." It was then that Caligari's smile faded and the interview came to an end. At the mention of the gallows, he refused to say any more. Caligari's testimony was complete.

Holmes stretched in his armchair. "Well, there you have it, Watson. It provides us with a little insight into the mind of this very disturbed man."

"Thank you, Holmes," I said. "The fellow sounds like a candidate for Bedlam rather than the noose."

"You are probably right, but I am sure that he will put up such an assured performance in the dock that the judge will have no option but to don the black cap. We shall see for ourselves, for no doubt we shall be called as witnesses. The trial will not take place for a few months, so for the moment our friend has been taken to Pentonville Prison, where a comfortable cell awaits him."

"I must say I was never more relieved to reach the conclusion of a case," I said with a heavy sigh. "Thank Heavens it is all over."

But I was wrong.

Chapter Thirty-three

Two months later

"Here he comes again," thought prison officer Arthur Brough, as he saw the now-familiar figure of Father Francis Smyth approach with that characteristic hobbling gait down the corridor. The long black cloak and large wide-brimmed hat were easily identifiable, even if the priest's rubicund features were somewhat masked by his headgear.

"Hello, my son," Father Smyth addressed Arthur, the voice a rich Irish brogue. "It seems it's always you on sentry duty when I come here to see my repentant sinner."

"So it does, Father. And you seem to be here nearly every day now."

"I do. I do. The poor man has little time left on God's earth and he needs all my help to make sure he has eased away all his blackest sins before he goes to meet his Maker. Never have I met a more contrite individual."

"If you say so, Father." Brough's voice was heavy with scepticism.

"So, my friend, if you'll open up the cell, I shall be about my ministry."

Brough nodded, retrieved a large key from the belt about his waist and unlocked the thick oak door to cell 31. The priest gave a nod of thanks and entered.

Brough closed the door and locked it, turning over in his mind as he did so certain phrases the priest had used: "repentant sinner", "contrite individual".

"My arse!" he muttered and spat vehemently onto the stone floor.

"And how are you today, my son?" asked Father Smyth of the prisoner.

Gustav Caligari gave a shrug. "I am coping, because I knew that you would visit me today. The time I spend with you gives me comfort and hope – hope of a peaceful end to my wretched life."

"It is not my doing, but God's comfort that gives you this ease."

Caligari nodded.

"Shall we pray together, my son?"

"That would please me tremendously."

The two men knelt on the floor of the cell and both intoned the Lord's Prayer. Then, taking Caligari's hands in his, Father Smyth said, "Do you remember the words of the prayer I taught you?"

Caligari nodded. "I have learned it by heart."

"Then let God hear it, my son."

Caligari lowered his head and spoke in a harsh whisper: "O Lord, Jesus Christ, Redeemer and Saviour, forgive my sins, just as You forgave Peter's denial and those who crucified You. Count not my transgressions, but, rather my tears of repentance. Remember not my iniquities, but, more especially, my sorrow for the offences I have committed against You. I long to be true to Your Word, and pray that You will love me and come to make Your dwelling place within me. I promise to give You praise and glory in love and in service all the days of my life."

The priest patted the prisoner on the back. "Words from the heart will be heard by the Almighty."

"That gives me comfort, despite the fact that there are so few days in my life remaining to me."

"But you will be safe in the knowledge that, as a true repentant sinner, you will be welcomed into the Kingdom of Heaven. Believe in the power of God's forgiveness and a great feeling of serenity will seep into your soul, my son."

"I am finding my situation easier to bear with each visit, but there is still a dark corner of my mind where the remembrance of my sins haunts and tortures me. I know I shall die soon, but I should like that dark corner to be eradicated before I do."

"Keeping praying and believing, and it will be so."

"You are a great comfort to me, Father. And there is little comfort in this lonely cell. I am allowed neither books nor writing materials. The only visitor I receive is you."

"How do you occupy your time, my son?"

Caligari gave a weak smile. "By using my imagination. By pretending that I am not in a dismal cell but elsewhere. I am on a hilltop overlooking green meadows, or in a fine house enjoying good company or dining in a splendid restaurant. With this latter thought in mind, I have used all my energies to shine the spoon they have provided me with to sup my gruel. See."

Caligari's hand reached into the thin straw of his mattress and produced a shiny spoon.

"It has taken me hours to get rid of the stains and grime. I have spat upon it, rubbed it with grit from the floor and polished it with the hem of my jacket. See now how it glimmers and shines in the light." Caligari held up the utensil before the priest's face, moving it gently from side to side.

"Wonderful, is it not, Father? So very, very wonderful. Bright, shiny and wonderful. Do you not think it is wonderful? So bright."

"Yes, yes," the priest responded slowly. "It is bright."

"See how it catches the dim light so that it sparkles – shines so brightly."

Caligari brought the spoon even closer to Father Smyth's face.

"See how it shines so brightly," he said softly.

"Yes," replied the priest dreamily, "it... does... shine... brightly... brightly."

Some fifteen minutes later Arthur Brough heard a loud knock at the door of cell 31.

"Hello there. We have finished in here," came the familiar Irish brogue.

Brough unlocked the door and released the cleric. "Another beneficial session, eh, Father?" he said sarcastically.

"Very beneficial indeed," replied the priest, pulling his hat even further down over his face and hobbling down the corridor on his way to the main door of the prison.

Chapter Thirty-four

ᐁ

From the journal of Dr. John H. Watson

Following the arrest of Caligari, I had the pleasure of informing Miss Ruth Marshall that she was no longer in danger and could resume her normal life. Holmes left me to deal with the matter. He was never very good at coping with emotional issues and avoided becoming involved in them whenever he could.

Her joy and delight at the news I was able to impart was dissipated by the revelation that her friend and fellow lodger, Blanche Andrews, had been murdered by the very creature who had attacked her.

"Oh, poor Blanche. That should have been me. She is dead because of me," she said, tears springing readily to her eyes.

"It is a tragedy," I agreed, "but at least you now know that you are no longer in any danger. The monster who carried out these heinous acts is on his way to the gallows. Any threat to your life has been removed."

She braved a smile. "And that is thanks to you and Mr. Holmes. Without your help and wise counsel – and of course Mrs. Hudson's kindness and hospitality – I don't know what would have happened."

I handed her into the care of Alan Firbank, who was equally delighted that Miss Marshall was free to resume a normal, unfettered life once more. We learned later, however, that her experiences in this dark affair had affected her more profoundly than she at first realised. She never did return to the stage. Her romance with Firbank faltered and shortly afterwards, she left London to find employment in the north of England.

About a month later, Holmes and I were passing a quiet evening in our Baker Street rooms, he cataloguing some new material in his criminal files and I leafing through the latest edition of *The Lancet*, when we were visited by Inspector Lestrade. He made another of his dramatic entrances. After one sharp knock at our door, he burst in upon us, red-faced and wild-eyed.

Holmes looked up languidly from his journal. "What news on the Rialto, Inspector? Something of a sensational nature, I deduce from the manner of your entrance."

"He's escaped. He's free. Caligari!"

"What!" exclaimed Holmes, papers slipping from his lap onto the floor. "How on earth did this happen?"

"The cunning devil," said Lestrade, mopping his damp brow with a lurid handkerchief. "Somehow he managed to hypnotise a priest who visited him in his cell and then escaped wearing his clothes."

Holmes gave a short, derisive laugh. "I warned you he was a devious cove, Lestrade, and needed more than the usual surveillance."

"We managed to trace him as far as Newhaven, where we lost him."

"No doubt he caught the ferry and has reached the Continent by now," I said.

"You almost have to admire him," observed Holmes. "The devil has remarkable qualities of ingenuity and resilience. It is a pity he employs them on the distaff of the law. Well, at least he is now out of your hair, Inspector. He is the concern of your European colleagues. We have played our part in this grim melodrama and now our revels are ended. I doubt he will return to these shores."

"You really think so, Holmes?" I said.

"I do. Why should he, when Europe offers such extensive hunting grounds? As I have observed on previous occasions, I am not the law; I merely represent justice as far as my feeble powers go. I shall keep in contact with my Continental colleagues; but, for the moment, I suspect that the fellow will have gone to earth. Nevertheless, I feel sure the world has not heard the last of Dr. Caligari and his murders."

Epilogue

From the journal of Dr. John H. Watson

Sherlock Holmes was correct in the assumption that we had not heard the last of Gustav Caligari. As my friend asserted, the villain never returned to England. Instead, however, he roamed Europe leaving behind him a trail of victims – unexplained, motiveless deaths in towns and villages across the Continent. Holmes believed that he had learned an important lesson while in this country. Given the nature of his murderous activities, it was dangerous to attempt to set up a permanent base in a single location, as Caligari had done in London. Remaining in one place made him vulnerable to suspicion and detection.

"It would be best if he were to adopt a gypsy life, never staying still for very long," observed my friend.

As usual, Holmes was correct. It was eventually established that Caligari had turned his hypnotist's talents into a travelling show, moving from fairground to fairground. Holmes kept a close watch on events and, with the assistance of information he provided, the authorities finally caught up with the villain at a fair in Holstenwall,

Germany, where he was running a sideshow with his latest somnambulist, a fellow called Cesare. Here he was arrested at last and incarcerated in a mental asylum; there, I believe, after falling into complete madness, he eventually perished.

Note

In order for a full account of the Caligari affair to be presented to the reader, the details of this narrative taken from Dr. Watson's journal have been supplemented by chapters based on interviews and records from the Holstenwall police bureau, medical notes recovered from the archives of the Brandt sanatorium for the insane in Düsseldorf and details from Caligari's diaries.

About the Author

D avid Stuart Davies is one of Britain's leading Sherlockian writers. He was editor of *Sherlock Holmes The Detective Magazine*, authored several Holmes novels, hit play *Sherlock Holmes: The Last Act*, Titan's *Starring Sherlock Holmes* and a biography of Jeremy Brett. He is advisor to the Sherlock Holmes museum, and contributed commentaries to DVDs of the Basil Rathbone Holmes films.

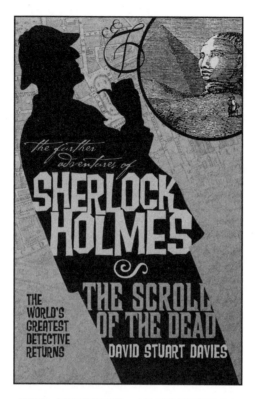

THE FURTHER ADVENTURES
OF SHERLOCK HOLMES

THE SCROLL OF THE DEAD

David Stuart Davies

In this fast-paced adventure, Sherlock Holmes attends a séance to
unmask an impostor posing as a medium. His foe, Sebastian Melmoth, is
a man hell-bent on discovering a mysterious Egyptian papyrus that may
hold the key to immortality. It is up to Holmes and Watson to use their
deductive skills to stop him or face disaster.

ISBN: 9781848564930

AVAILABLE NOW!

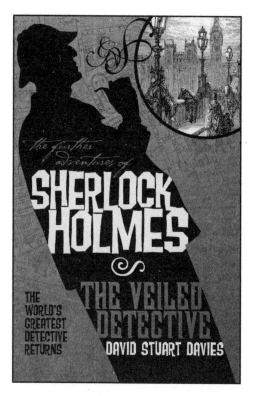

THE FURTHER ADVENTURES
OF SHERLOCK HOLMES

THE VEILED DETECTIVE

David Stuart Davies

It is 1880, and a young Sherlock Holmes arrives in London to pursue a
career as a private detective. He soon attracts the attention of criminal
mastermind Professor James Moriarty, who is driven by his desire to
control this fledgling genius. Enter Dr. John H. Watson, soon to make
history as Holmes' famous companion.

ISBN: 9781848564909

AVAILABLE NOW!

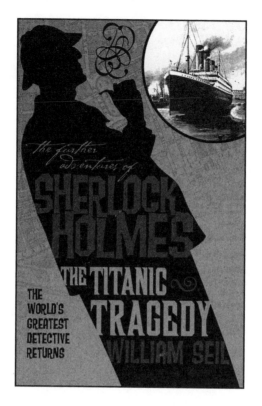

THE FURTHER ADVENTURES
OF SHERLOCK HOLMES

THE TITANIC TRAGEDY

William Seil

Holmes and Watson board the *Titanic* in 1912, where Holmes is to carry
out a secret government mission. Soon after departure, highly important
submarine plans for the U.S. navy are stolen. Holmes and Watson work
through a list of suspects which includes Colonel James Moriarty, brother to
the late Professor Moriarty—will they find the culprit before tragedy strikes?

ISBN: 9780857687104

AVAILABLE NOW!

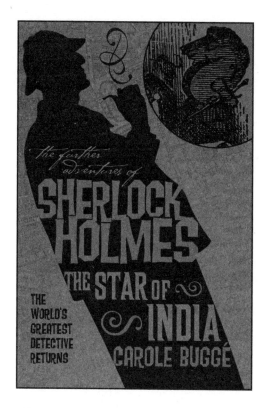

THE FURTHER ADVENTURES
OF SHERLOCK HOLMES

THE STAR OF INDIA

Carole Buggé

Holmes and Watson find themselves caught up in a complex chessboard
of a problem, involving a clandestine love affair and the disappearance
of a priceless sapphire. Professor James Moriarty is back to tease and
torment, leading the duo on a chase through the dark and dangerous
back streets of London and beyond.

ISBN: 9780857681218

AVAILABLE NOW!

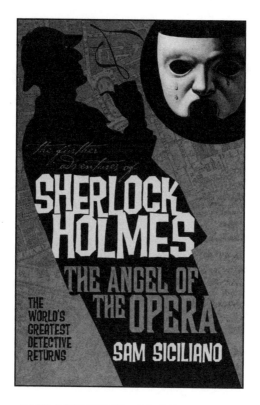

THE FURTHER ADVENTURES
OF SHERLOCK HOLMES

THE ANGEL OF THE OPERA

Sam Siciliano

Paris, 1890. Sherlock Holmes is summoned across the English Channel
to the famous Opera House. Once there, he is challenged to discover
the true motivations and secrets of the notorious phantom, who rules its
depths with passion and defiance.

ISBN: 9781848568617

AVAILABLE NOW!